THE SHEIKH'S BARGAIN BRIDE

DESERT KINGS, BOOK 2

DIANA FRASER

BAY BOOKS

The Sheikh's Bargain Bride
by Diana Fraser

© 2011 Diana Fraser
Print Edition
ISBN: 978-0992259129

The ultimate controlling sheikh, Zahir Al-Zaman is so obsessed with freedom-loving Anna Whitman that he traps her into marriage. But he won't force her into his bed; he has his strategies for seduction.

Despite an intense attraction, Anna refuses to be seduced because she won't have a relationship based on lies. But how can she reveal secrets that will destroy the beliefs he holds most dear?

—Desert Kings—
Wanted: A Wife for the Sheikh
The Sheikh's Bargain Bride
The Sheikh's Lost Lover
Awakened by the Sheikh
Claimed by the Sheikh
Wanted: A Baby by the Sheikh

You can sign up to Diana's newsletter via her website for information on book releases.

For more information about this author, visit:
http://www.dianafraser.net

This is a work of fiction. Names, characters, places, and incidents are the product of the author's imagination, and are used fictitiously. Any resemblance to actual events, locales or persons, living or dead, is co-incidental. All rights reserved. Except as permitted under the US Copyright Act of 1976, no part of this publication may be reproduced, distributed or transmitted in any form or by any means, or stored in a database or retrieval system, without prior permission of the author.

CHAPTER 1

Sheikh Zahir al-Zaman narrowed his eyes against the glare of the sun-bleached stony plains and focused on the slowly materializing dark speck. Within minutes the helicopter's low rhythmic thrum filled the overcast spring sky like an angry locust intent on devastation.

She hadn't wasted any time. But then he'd made sure she couldn't refuse his invitation. He banished a flicker of discomfort with practiced ease. Sometimes you had to lure the prey to you. Sometimes, in a way that wasn't palatable.

But the ends always justified the means. She *would* be his and he was prepared to do whatever it took to make it happen.

He watched the helicopter alight in a cloud of dust before the palace. The pilot lifted out a small case and began to open the door before it was pushed open abruptly from within and two long, jean-clad legs emerged. A tall blonde jumped down and looked around the palace, her head twisting and turning impatiently.

She'd changed. She was thinner, her hair longer, her face no longer sun-kissed but as pale as the desert under moonlight. Still, his body responded the same to her now, as it did when she visited him in his dreams.

He'd lived with his obsession with her for six long years: cursing and nurturing the anger at her deceit and betrayal while still longing to relive the passion of their one night together. But his brother's death meant he no longer had to live with the madness.

Then, with an imperceptible movement of her head, she looked up and saw him. Zahir frowned and his breath caught unexpectedly in his chest. Ice blue eyes stared at him, challenging him, demanding an explanation from him. How could eyes so cool and northern spark such fire? She turned away suddenly and slid the door of the helicopter shut with a force that belied her fragility. The metallic crash echoed around the palace, destroying its peace and order.

He'd get what he wanted but he knew, without a doubt, that it wasn't going to be easy.

"You are to wait here. The sheikh is busy at present but he will see you when he is free."

"No way!" Anna threw down her bag onto the nearest chair. "I don't care if he's with the President of the United States. Tell him I'm here and tell him I *will* see him immediately."

The Bedu servant simply nodded and withdrew from the room.

Anna strode across the vast, stone-flagged reception hall, threw open the wooden shutters of the nearest window and looked out, searching for any signs of her son in the tiled courtyard below. There were none.

She turned her gaze up to the lofty ceiling, its ornately carved pillars and beams shrouded in shadows, and tried to hold back the despair and grief that filled her.

Zahir, you bastard, where's my son?

He knew she'd arrived. She'd seen him watching her from above. She had a sixth sense where he was concerned, where anyone was concerned if they threatened her or her child.

She raked her hair into a fresh ponytail and smoothed down her shirt. As much to give her trembling hands something to do as to prepare herself for the meeting.

But her hands continued to shake as her body readied itself for a confrontation. She sat down in the nearest chair and gathered her anger to her. It had been anger that had stopped the fear from taking over. And she needed it now.

A month with only phone and Skype calls to her son and now so near but still she couldn't get to him. She could scream with frustration and something else that she tried to ignore. It made her skin prickle, it made her feel sick to her stomach. She dropped her head in her hands and took a deep breath in order to control it. But despite her best efforts it would not be beaten. Fear was like that. And she was scared now. Scared of losing her son.

The smooth slide of soft leather sandals alerted her to the return of the servant. She looked up into the weathered face of the old Bedu expectantly.

"This way, madam."

Her booted footsteps rang loudly on the ancient stone corridors, worn smooth by the footsteps of generations of the al-Zaman dynasty. They walked for what seemed like an age through beautifully proportioned rooms that unfolded one on to another, down echoing colonnaded walkways that skirted magnificent gardens, past perfumed courtyards and mysterious corridors that seemed to disappear directly into the rocky hillside upon which the palace was built.

At last the Bedu servant opened a heavy set of dark teak doors.

"You may wait here."

She stepped into the room and looked around, awed despite herself.

The room was obviously part of the less formal wing of the palace. While it bore the same marks of antiquity as the grand reception hall, it possessed none of its austerity. Here, light from high clerestory windows warmed the sandstone rock and imbued the amber and creams of the tiled wall with a magical glow. She could hear the splash of a fountain coming from the courtyard beyond the open windows and she could smell sweet jasmine.

It was furnished for comfort too, with simple, over-sized suede sofas in neutral tones grouped around a huge wooden table, glowing with a patina created from years of care.

She sat down wearily and looked around. It was a room designed to appeal to the senses: a seductive room. God help her.

She dropped her bag and her hand instinctively caressed the geometric inlay that edged the wooden table. It was smooth, worn by generations of hands seeking to engage with its beauty. But even as her fingers sought the same engagement, her eyes searched the shadows.

A cool breeze alerted her to a door opening on the far side of the room, behind a wooden screen.

She didn't see him at first but she knew he was there. Just the feel of his powerful presence close by kick-started something deep inside that had lain dormant since she'd seen him last. Her heart hammered against her chest and she could feel heat rise through her body that had nothing to do with the warmth of the spring afternoon.

Then he emerged, all dark and light. There had never been any half measures with Zahir—physically, intellectually, or emotionally. It had been a part of the initial attraction to be with someone so *definite*, so *sure*. Now, the white of his robes accentuated the rich nutmeg of his skin and the shadows that gathered below the strong lines of his face. His eyes, too, seemed to absorb the light. They held no subtlety of expression or color, only intensity.

She felt that intensity connect with her at an elemental level, just as it had when they met nearly six years ago. It was the same as before except for the cold control that she could sense within him and except for the fact that she was a mother now with more to lose than herself.

Then he moved forward into the light and the impression evaporated. He was the powerful, charismatic sheikh still, but civilized. While a smile curled at his lips, his eyes showed reserve, distance.

"*Salamm w aleykum,* Anna." He nodded to her in greeting. "How was your journey? I hope my staff were attentive?"

She jumped up. "Where is he?"

"Surely that is no way to greet your brother-in-law? Not in my country, nor yours, I believe."

"It's the way we treat people—family or not—who are trying to take their child away from them."

"I agree, such circumstances don't warrant the usual courtesies. However, I am old-fashioned in such things."

"Spare me the lecture in manners and tell me where I can find my son. We'll be leaving on the next plane out."

"Please sit. I have ordered you mint tea. Is that satisfactory?"

"Where is he?"

He smiled and sat down.

"Anna. I am being polite. I am asking questions that you should, in turn, answer politely. Didn't your mother…? No. Of course not. From the little Abdullah told me about you it would seem your upbringing in the so-called 'civilized' United States was far from my own idea of civilized. It would appear that all you managed to glean from your mother was a desire for wealth." His eyes glittered. "And you managed to achieve that well enough, didn't you? Managed to dupe my romantic brother easily enough."

"Stop right there. I haven't traveled nearly seven thousand miles to pretend we're on polite terms. I want my son. God knows how much money it took for you to get the court to rule that he come here for a holiday. And how much more to keep him here." She smoothed her hand over her tightly-bound hair. "Where is he?"

At the thought of her son she could feel tears prick her eyelids and the maelstrom of emotions that churned in her heart threaten to surface. But still she determinedly held his gaze. He *would* tell her where to find her son and she *would* not weaken.

When the court had made its decision she'd been forced to concede to Matta having a fortnight's holiday in Qawaran without her. She'd survive. And she knew Matta would enjoy the time with his father's family who he knew well from frequent visits to the States. And he'd have his beloved nurse with him. But the weeks had drawn out into a month and she'd been forced to seek a visa to come to find her son, terrified he'd never be returned to her. And she was here, now to make sure he was.

He sat back and looked her slowly up and down, from her well-worn boots to her hair that hadn't seen a stylist in months. Well, what of it? She stood straight and eyed him directly. She might have married a wealthy man but, since her husband's death, she was wealthy no longer.

"Anna." It was his gentle tone that did it. She felt the pain crack through the anger that was her shield. She turned away but not before she saw the reaction to her anguish revealed in his face.

"Anna, my nephew is with Muma Yemena, resting before dinner."

She nodded, trying to control her leap of excitement at getting through to him. "He's well?"

"Of course. He's been well cared for. Muma Yemena has been his nurse since birth."

"Only because you insisted. At five years old he doesn't need a nurse."

"It is our custom. And it also ensured he was kept in touch with his culture."

She sighed and sat down, studying her hands in her lap, all fight gone. She was trying desperately to control the gnawing fear that her son no longer needed her.

"I want to see him now." Her voice was edgy, nervous.

"Not yet."

She jumped up. "If you don't take me to him, I'll find him myself."

He shook his head. "You'd be lost within minutes."

She turned and headed for the door. But before she could open it he was beside her, his hands gripping her wrists.

"Anna. You need to calm down before you see him. We have to talk first."

"You have two minutes and then I'm off."

She froze as he tightened his grip around her hand.

"I'll take as long as I like and you *will* listen."

"What the hell do we have to say to each other that hasn't already been said? What else do you need to know?"

"I? I don't need to know anything further. But you do."

Her voice was quiet. "I hate you Zahir. You made it clear at Abduallah's funeral that you wouldn't rest until you could bring Matta to Qawaran. And you were as good as your word. But his visit is over. He's coming back to the US with me today."

"You still don't understand do you? Matta is here because he will be living with me from now on."

"No!" She shook her head, tiny little shakes that sent

tremors through her body. "I will never let Matta stay here with you. You have no legal rights."

"I am his uncle. He will be my heir. He will have everything. With you, he will have nothing. Hardly the doting mother to deprive your child of so much."

"A child needs his mother. For God's sake. There must be some shadow of humanity in you. Think of your own mother. Think of her."

"My mother died when Abduallah was a baby and when I was ten. I scarcely remember her. A child needs to learn early to survive and Matta will do just that."

"No! You can't take him. Any court in any country would give the mother custody of her own child."

"Depends on what can be proved against the mother."

"Nothing. You have *nothing* against me. I have done *nothing*."

The thin veneer of politeness left him instantly. The seductive silky-smooth aura of the wealthy womanizer—whose playground knew no borders, no limits—was replaced by the powerful sheikh who'd spent his younger life at war where no rules applied. The change was in his eyes. They were bare—stripped of the chill aloofness—naked and fierce.

"You've done *everything*. Abduallah is *dead* because of you and your family."

She shook her head. But she was unable to completely deny the connection between her family and the death of Abduallah. If she hadn't introduced him to her brother; if the drugs hadn't been so readily available to someone with her brother's connections and Abduallah's money...

But it wasn't her. She couldn't be held responsible. "No." She shook her head more strongly.

"Face facts, Anna, you're hardly the virtuous widow. Evidence can easily be obtained."

"You wouldn't."

"What? Fabricate evidence against you? I don't need to. It's surprising how easily people talk—say whatever you want them to—when money is involved. I know that you're not a drug user—never have been—but your connections proved fatal to Abduallah. And, believe me, I'd do anything to secure the future of my own flesh and blood."

She blanched at his words. "Matta?"

"Of course."

"Matta is *my* son," she repeated. "I'm not giving him to you: not now, not ever. I'd die before that happened."

He stepped toward her, scanning her face. She had nowhere to go. Her back was already pressed against the door. He touched her cheek with his finger, softly drawing down a velvety trail that ended at her jaw. He narrowed his eyes at the sight of the moisture on his fingertip. She hadn't even known she was crying.

The crease between his brows deepened. He swung round as if to turn away, as if to mask some inner struggle, but stopped abruptly and turned back to face her. Silently his eyes searched hers and she saw the chill had gone, replaced by a complex intensity that confused her.

"You love him then," he said dully.

"The word 'love' sounds strange on your lips, Zahir. I'm surprised you know what it means."

He dropped the hand that hovered close to her cheek, his handsome face suddenly weary. Abduallah had told her of Zahir's sacrifice: the years of desert warfare, living away from home in order to protect his family and country. How could a man, so isolated, so accustomed to war, know anything about love?

"Tell me, Anna, why did you marry my brother?"

His question caught her off-guard. She hesitated as she remembered the brief courtship with her husband—so different to that of the other men she'd known.

"He was gentle; he respected me." Even as she uttered the words she realized how impossibly small they must sound to people who didn't have to fight for everything they had. But, to her, they had been huge—big enough to divert her from her hard-won Cornell scholarship. Abduallah had wanted her to travel with him. He was always restless for new things and she'd been young and too easily persuaded. She'd never make that mistake again.

"That's it? You've put our family through hell because you needed respect?"

"I married him because I loved him."

His gaze fell briefly. He walked away and looked through one of the huge domed windows with views across the desert, out to the distant red hills.

"Loved his money more. It must have seemed a miracle that someone of his standing should take interest in someone like you."

His bitter tone and the injustice of it all got to her. "Why? You did," she snapped back.

She bit her lip. Referring to their one-night stand was hardly clever in the present circumstances.

He slowly turned to face her. Horizontal beams of late afternoon sunlight shone onto his dark face but revealed nothing. He was like a closed book now as he approached her.

Closed and too close.

A muscle flickered in his jaw.

"I," he flicked loose the band that held her hair back and watched intently as it swung into position like a curtain of silk, "knew nothing about you that night. Least of all that you were married to my brother. Besides, I am not my brother. I am a realist. I harbor no sentimental illusions about anything or anyone. I suggest you remember that."

She grabbed the band from his hand. "And I suggest you show me some respect."

"If it's respect you want I suggest you try practicing loyalty, try speaking the truth."

"Things"—she hesitated as she rejected the words of defense that sprung to her lips—"are never as simple as they appear." There was no point in elaborating. Whatever she said, she was damned in his eyes.

"It was *exactly* that simple."

She sensed the latent power of his fist as it ground briefly against the doorframe before he turned away.

She had no fear for herself. She knew instinctively that he would never hurt her physically. It was what he could do to her emotionally that scared her.

"There's only one simple fact here and that's that Matta is *my* son and he will *not* be living here with you."

He turned to face her, all signs of his anger masked once more. He shook his head. "The child stays." His lips quirked into a chilling smile.

The chill turned to ice down her spine and destroyed all hope.

"You can't take him away from me. You can't." She stepped toward him and clutched his arm in desperation, gathering the loose folds of his robe like a dying woman gripping tight to a lifeline. He stilled instantly as if electrified. His eyes were lowered, in disdain, she imagined. But she had nothing left. "What do I have to do to make you see?"

"You can do nothing." He raised his hand slowly to hers, still clutching the soft silk of his robe, and then pressed it against hers. For one long moment she thought she might have got through—touched something inside of him—but then his hand grasped hers and dragged it away. "Begging won't get you anywhere."

"Then what will?" He was silent and she pressed her

advantage. She had nothing to lose and everything to gain. "Zahir, you can't take him. He's my life." She shook her head and he closed his eyes briefly as her hair swept his cheek. He trapped a strand between his fingers but didn't let it fall.

"And what is your life to me? Life in the desert, life at war, is worth only what it can be bargained for. What," he added softly, "would you give in return for your son?"

"You want to bargain?" she asked, incredulous.

"Yes."

"What do you want?"

"You."

He let his hand trail down her arm.

"Why would you possibly want me when you have so little respect for me."

He smiled. "Respect? More like unfinished business."

Something, fear or lust, sliced through her deep inside and sent shivers radiating out to her skin. He lifted her hand and examined her forearm, now raised with goosebumps.

"Cold, Anna?"

"Disgusted, Zahir."

"I think not. I think, I know, you want me still. If you live with me, here in Qarawan, you can still be with your son. Otherwise, you will never see him again."

"You can't do this."

"I have the power, Anna, believe me. Now, you have my conditions, what is your answer?"

"Let's get this straight. You want me for sex and in return I can live with my son? You're a twisted man."

"I am an honorable man. I will not force myself on you. You will come to me soon enough."

She shook her head. "Never."

"Six years ago I had to merely enter the room and you wanted me. You could barely wait to get me in the elevator, in the hotel room before your hands found my bare skin, before they explored my body, unzipped my trousers, and before your lips—"

"Stop!"

"How many times did we make love that night, Anna?" His voice had dropped to a roughened whisper.

She swallowed hard and felt a surge of heat rise with the pounding of her heart and a dull ache of longing settle between her legs. It was true. She'd wanted him then and she wanted him now.

She shook her head helplessly. "I can't remember."

"I think you can. I think you do remember; I think you relive those moments because, like you, I can't forget them either. You *will* come to me. Make no mistake."

He was so close now that she could feel the quickened rise of his chest rub against her breasts, could feel the seductive slide of his silk robe brush her skin. Unable to meet his gaze, she kept her eyes lowered, focused on his mouth, on lips so soft, so utterly at odds with the rest of him that they conjured up images she was desperate to forget.

She could see that he knew where her thoughts led by the smile that gently quirked those soft lips.

"You see? The needs of your body are greater than anything else. You want me and you shall have me."

"How can you do this?"

He continued as if he hadn't heard her words. "And then, you will also have your child. Only this time, I will not be your husband's inconvenient brother. I will be your husband."

"You want me to marry you?"

"Of course. Marriage is the only respectable way. We have my heir, your son, to consider remember."

"But you don't love me. Why marry me?"

"You are from the West. Marriage is not for life—surely you know that—and nowhere more so than in my country.

When I tire of you I may take another wife. Or simply remove you to another palace. It is not a problem."

"*You* are an immoral bastard."

"That's no way to talk about your future husband."

"And *you*, such as *you*, want to be the father of my child."

"I will care for him. He is of my blood."

They were close now, their eyes trained on each other, holding both the power of attraction that had originally brought them together and the anger and bitterness that had followed. She could feel his breath quicken against her cheek, as he must have felt hers.

"No." The single, despairing word floated between them —too soft to be of any real show of force against him.

"Yes." His voice was also soft—he had no need to prove anything. He moved even closer to her, until there was nothing between the two of them. No separation and no escape.

He dipped his head to hers, as if to inhale her and her breath caught.

In that one instant she absorbed the details of his face as if she could actually *feel* the dark stubble of his jaw roughly abrading her own jaw, could *feel* his silky hair fall gently against her own cheek. She closed her eyes in order to break the connection, willing herself to dispel the confusion of hate and need; the clash between mind and body.

When she re-opened them he'd stepped away, a defiant weariness in place.

"Come, you need to rest and then I will have Matta brought to you."

She shook her head as if to free it of the nightmare that was unfolding. He was right. She had only one choice left open to her. She felt herself literally crumple then. Her legs buckled under her and all fight vanished.

Suddenly she felt his arm around her, steadying her, giving her the strength she needed.

"It will not be so bad, Anna. You will have everything you need, more than you could imagine. You will be gaining far more than you will be leaving behind."

She pushed him away. "You know nothing. All I would be gaining would be my child. I would be losing everything else that I've treasured and worked toward my whole adult life."

He swung open the double doors and stood back for her to pass.

"What could you possibly be leaving behind that you treasure so much?"

She walked out into the warm light of the evening sun and looked away, far away, out to the distant mountains now a bluish haze against a soft apricot sky.

"My independence."

The hollow echo of the banging doors swallowed her words. She doubted he'd even heard them.

CHAPTER 2

Anna watched the shadows slowly take form as the soft pre-dawn light revealed her bedroom in all its luxurious detail. Although ancient, it seemed everything in the palace had been designed to seduce the senses: from the fine, white silk curtains that shimmered in the fresh breeze, to the fragrance of the orange blossom that lingered in the air like an invitation.

But there was only one luxury that was a necessity. And he was now curled up in her arms. She sighed with pleasure and shifted her arm gently from underneath Matta's head and looked down on her sleeping son in awe.

Relaxed, his arms were flung either side of his head and his feet had kicked off the light covers. With the same rich, skin tones as his father, he looked as though he belonged amidst the exotic surroundings that were so strange to her eyes.

The thought twisted in her gut, creating a void she knew might never be filled. He was moving away from her. From the moment they'd been reunited, the previous evening, she'd seen that he was at home here in the palace. He'd heard the stories and poetry of Qawaran growing up and even knew a few words of the country's language. Watching him run around, followed by a doting army of extended family and servants, she'd seen him settled in a way he'd never been before.

Once more, her eyes absorbed his plump cheeks and the dark-fringed lids, lying in a peaceful crescent on his dark skin. She'd do anything to give him the best life possible. Even if it meant admitting Zahir was right. Perhaps this was where her son needed to be, where he belonged. As heir to the kingdom of Qawaran he would have a life of power and privilege. If she robbed him of that, would he forgive her later? Would her middle-class suburban American life be enough for him? She shook her head in despair. Truth was, she couldn't compete with what Zahir offered him.

She shivered and rose from the bed, drawn to the huge eastern window framed by once bold carvings that had been muted by the touch of generations. The window held an expansive view of the endless stony hammada plains contained by a horizon that was a mere charcoal line in the colorless, pre-dawn light.

It was a raw view of infinite monotony but yet of infinite power. It was mesmerizing.

She settled onto the window seat, pushed open the ancient lead-paned window and leaned out, gazing up at the austere walls of the palace. Where the palace began and the rock face ended was anybody's guess. The palace and the rocky escarpment rose high above the plains, seemingly one, belying the luxury found within.

A suggestion of a shadow passed over her in the pale light and she looked up to the top-most crags that peaked high above the castle. A huge falcon wheeled silently in the high, eddying winds, lost in a world of casual freedom.

Only something that had never been held captive could take freedom so lightly. She would not take it so lightly.

"Mom!" Matta's softly rounded body jumped into her lap, his arms lifting to wrap himself around her body. He trusted her implicitly and she had to think of him, not her. What *she* wanted had to be secondary.

She caressed his back gently and Matta's breathing slowed and with his cheek pressed to her chest he sighed, a deep, contented sigh, and immediately fell asleep again. Anna's mind drifted to Abduallah. Despite appearances, she knew Abduallah had never been truly happy in the West. And if he'd stayed in Qawaran, who knows, he might still be alive. She hated to admit it but Zahir was right. Matta's place was here, in Qawaran.

She looked back down at Matta's sleep-flushed cheeks, gently pushed away a lock of dark hair, and kissed his head. And she knew that wherever Matta was, she would be also.

∽

ZAHIR SAT BACK, took a third sip of the coffee and passed the dallah to Anna who, like him, sat cross-legged, her robes falling loosely around her slim frame.

If she was surprised at the traditional ceremony, at the sharing of a cup, of the strong, cardamom-flavored coffee, then she hid it well. His eyes followed her lips as they pressed to the small, white cup, the soft vertical lines slightly pursed as she sipped the hot coffee.

Had her face, her lips, always been so delicate? His time with her had been intense but brief. He didn't recall the translucence of her skin with the dark smudges under her eyes and he didn't remember her lips, from which he'd felt nothing but power, being so finely drawn.

"So, was the bargain—such as it is—a good one?" She

looked up suddenly as she spoke, her blond hair—white blond in places—shimmering around her face and he could see that her blue-gray eyes still held that same look of strength and challenge. "You're checking me over like I'm some kind of possession. Just wondered if you think you've got your money's worth."

"Of course. I wouldn't have struck the bargain otherwise."

"Oh I think you would. I don't think you care one bit how I've changed. You want me to give you everything and you to give me nothing in return." She grunted. "Some bargain."

He shrugged. "I'm allowing you to remain with your son. That is what you want, isn't it?"

She glared at him. "You know it is."

"Then I assume you agree to stay."

"Why? Why do you want me to? Just tell me why. You've said yourself you don't believe mothers are necessary. So why do you want me to stay? Why do you want us to marry?"

"I've told you. It's seemly; it's proper. There's no more to be said."

"I think there is. I think there's a lot more to it. You're trying to punish me somehow aren't you? You believe me to be responsible for your brother's death. You're punishing me for betraying him with you, that night so long ago."

He didn't speak immediately. Punishment? Maybe a little. He watched her emotions flicker across her gray-blue eyes and felt the familiar arousal he felt every time he thought of her, dreamed of her. But she was here, now, in the flesh and his feelings were ten times what they were. She had to know the truth.

"Why do I want you? It is simple. I have spent every day of the last six years imagining making love to you; remembering your eyes, your mouth, open, moist, wanting. Your thighs, how they felt against my tongue, against my fingers."

He paused briefly, arrested by the sight of her shocked

expression as he took her back to the memory of their one night together. Her hand was frozen in the act of raising the coffee cup to her lips: lips, he noticed, that were lightly parted as if spellbound by his words. And her gaze held his with eyes that had become more violet than blue from the inner heat of arousal that he could see shimmering across her skin.

He smiled to himself. He simply had to give her time for her mind to allow what her body already knew.

"I cannot live like that," he continued. "I have work to do, a people and a country to govern. I must have you to rid myself of this obsession."

She took a deep breath as she placed the coffee cup carefully before her. "And how exactly do you propose to have me? You said that it would not be by force. Or have you changed your mind on that score?"

"You insult me. I would never do anything so dishonorable."

"So let's get this straight. You'd practically kidnap my son and blackmail me into marriage. And that's not dishonorable?"

"No. That is a means to an end. Taking you by force would have no positive benefits, other than temporary. It is you," he looked into her eyes, "who I must have. And it must be done willingly or it will be ineffective."

"Zahir. You're like a spoiled boy, wanting only what you can't have. You think like one too. Once you get it then you won't want it anymore. I'll be moved to a corner of the palace and forgotten about."

"You understand perfectly."

She shook her head. "I won't play your games."

"Why not? Come to me. Let us ride out this mutual obsession," he held up his hand to silence her. "It *is* mutual. And then it will be over."

Over. Could she do it? Swallow her pride and her dreams and give in to his wishes? But not just to *his* wishes, she was forced to admit. Her mind had been desperately trying to control her physical response to Zahir since she'd entered the room. And she'd succeeded at first. But his words of passion broke through that control, filling her mind with nothing but the memory of the heat of his naked body against hers, of the rhythmic movement of his hips as he drove into her repeatedly, sending her over the edge to a place that she dared not revisit. Without control she would be entirely at his mercy.

"I can see you like the thought."

She could feel her cheeks burning.

"I won't make it so easy for you."

"Easy for *you*, I would have thought. Lie with me, then, when the obsession is vented—maybe months, maybe years —it will be over. You can do whatever you wish to do: stay here with Matta, or not. You will be wealthy and have the freedom and independence you claim you've left behind."

So he had heard her. And yet he'd made no sign or acknowledgment of her words last night.

His flippant use of the words that she held so dear angered her. What did he know about growing up, always on the outside of society, looking in? What did he know about studying all night in order to gain the education that she knew to be the key to independence? What did he know about letting her own dreams slip away from her, shifting them to her son? Matta *would* be loved. He would be a part of this world that had excluded her from birth, by virtue *of* her birth.

"I will keep my end of the bargain. I will marry you and live here, for one reason only—to be with my son. But I will not sleep with you, Zahir."

He shrugged. "I am used to battles, to strategy, I will get

what I want. It will maybe take a little longer. But there is something to be said for the anticipation."

"This is a battle you will not win."

"Ah, Anna, I have fought many battles and lost none. A knowledge of one's opponent is vital."

She passed the cup back to Zahir.

"The outcome doesn't bode well for you then, does it? You don't know me at all."

"But I do. I know that there is a reason for your outwardly conciliatory behavior. You are wearing Qawarian robes; you are partaking in the ancient Bedu coffee ceremony without comment. You are doing this *not* because it is easy for you, because it is familiar. You are doing it for a reason."

And Anna had no intention of telling Zahir the real reason why she preferred to wear clothes that were like a uniform, which hid her and made her anonymous.

"I have no problems adapting to other people's cultures. I was brought up amongst people of all nationalities. You could say I had an early education in world culture and cuisine."

If you could call scavenging food from the back door of different restaurants in downtown Pittsburgh—Italian, Spanish, Chinese, Mexican—an education, then yes, her taste buds were educated all right. Educated in getting something for nothing, in survival.

"I know more about you than you think. I understand your childhood was, shall we say, 'interesting.'"

"I know what you're saying, Zahir. You despise my background and, you know what? I don't blame you because I didn't much like it myself. But I tried to do something about that." She couldn't go on, her voice faltered and tears threatened the mask she was trying to keep on her emotions.

"And you failed, didn't you. Married, became pregnant,

and let your own weak need for 'respect' and 'love' prevent you from escaping that world. You see, every opponent has a weakness. And I know yours."

He was watching her closely, waiting to see if she would take the bait. She looked down briefly. "You can think what you like."

"There, again, you are holding back. You are not wanting an argument, you are waiting, watching." He smiled as he acknowledged the truth in her face. "That is the measure of a good tactician."

"It is the measure of someone with no other resources than to wait and discover how, exactly, you aim to seduce me. I'm sure, like everything else, you have it planned."

"Indeed."

"Then what is your strategy?"

"I have fought many battles and have never found it in my interests to reveal my strategies before battle commenced."

"Battle." She repeated, nodding, her lips pursed with restraint. "I guess anything goes in a battle, then. Tricks, treachery—"

"And skill, don't forget skill."

She looked up quickly and caught the heat of his gaze. There was no doubt he was skilled. She remembered his skills vividly.

"It's a game to you, isn't it? Listen, Zahir, there's only one reason I'm here, and that's for Matta."

"You have to face facts, Anna. There is little you can give the boy. He has everything he needs here. One of my sisters and her children live here and will give him companionship. He will receive only the best education and care. His nurse, Muma Yemena, will ensure that he—"

"*He* has a name—"

"Will be cared for."

"She's his nurse not his mom!"

"She was my brother's nurse, and then Matta's. And she is also a dutiful and loyal Arab woman and will help Matta adapt to his new home."

"A boy needs his mother. A dutiful and loyal Arab woman isn't enough. You underestimate the power of a mother's love."

"No." He paused. "I don't. I've made sure he has his mother, have I not?"

"Through blackmail, yes."

Zahir shrugged. "You are both here, that is what matters. Come"—Zahir stood up—"I will take you back to your rooms."

"It's not necessary. I'm sure you've business to attend."

"I have cancelled everything over the next few weeks except for an important meeting later this morning. That, I must attend alone."

"A few weeks. You think that will be enough time?"

"To seduce you? Of course."

THEY WALKED SILENTLY through ancient passages supported by arches that soared high into the ceiling, one arch following another until they faded into the pale gold of the sandstone.

Despite the fact it seemed such an alien world to Anna, she couldn't help be awed by it. She felt a sense of peace settle within her, as if the very walls emanated a strength absorbed from the people who had lived and loved and died there over countless centuries. Somehow its power seeped under her skin and calmed the frustrating blend of anger and arousal that simply being with Zahir sparked.

"I imagine Abduallah spoke to you of the palace?"

"A little. He described its beauty but I never imagined it would be like this."

"It is more than merely beautiful. It is a symbol of my people, of the strength that lies in their culture and tradition, of the importance of loyalty and duty." He stopped in front of a heavy latticed door and turned to her. "Such things are still important today, don't you think?"

Gone were the accusations and chilling control of the day before. Instead, his expression looked curious, as if he was genuinely interested in her reply.

"Depends on one's culture and tradition. Some people need to escape their 'family traditions' and find their own way in the world." She shrugged, trying to appear nonchalant, trying not to remember her own desperate need to escape her family's downward spiral. "Not much chance of escape from here though."

"The palace is about security, not escape. Come." He opened the door into an exquisite courtyard garden. It was smaller than the others they'd passed, with a perfectly round white marble fountain surrounded by a jasmine-covered pergola, fragrant citrus, and subtly colored paths. It was the garden upon which her bedroom opened.

"My suite of rooms is opposite yours."

She hadn't realized that.

The intimate privacy of the garden and his proximity unsettled her. She was very aware of the earthy notes of his aftershave mingling with the heady jasmine.

She moved away from him, over to the fountain, desperate to clear her head of him. She sat on its polished, gleaming edge and plunged both hands into the water. She cupped the crystal clear water in her palms and brought it to her face. She could almost swear it had a fragrance, of something sweet and pure. She let the water trickle through her fingers.

"Spring water." He was suddenly there beside her, watching her intently. She kept her eyes fixed on the water, but aware of every movement, every ripple in his gown. "Drawn from deep in the mountains. It's been the life force of the palace and its community for centuries. *Ma-ush-shafa*."

"Healing water." She streaked her hands through the water, watching the sun sparkle in its midst, remembering her husband's love of poetry and the Koran. If Zahir was the fighter in the family, her husband, Abduallah, had been the poet. He used to read aloud to her, revealing his love for the country that he could never return to. Shame bit too deep. He couldn't face his family. She suddenly realized Zahir had been silent for a few minutes. She looked up.

Zahir held her gaze for one long, unfathomable moment before turning away abruptly.

"I must go. I have business to attend. You will stay here and we will dine later—"

"I am not one of your servants to order—"

"And Matta is here. Be with him until my business is complete."

She looked around startled—she hadn't heard Matta approach—and suddenly he was in her arms once more. His old nurse and young cousins, Zahir's sister's children, hovered on the edge of the garden, awaiting permission to enter.

By the time she'd freed her arms and beckoned them to come, Zahir had gone.

By late afternoon, Matta was asleep and Anna was free to wander the corridors, gardens, and rooms of the palace alone. She found herself on one of the upper levels, looking down on the entrance to the palace. It must have been from here that Zahir had watched her arrive only the day before. It felt like weeks. Now it was her turn to watch as Zahir bid his Bedu guests a formal farewell.

They were a fearsome sight: belts filled with gun cartridges; rifles held as naturally in their hands as if they were briefcases; heavily-engraved silver daggers thrust under their belts. Their white robes gleamed in the harsh sunlight, a stark contrast to their dark, weathered skin. Despite the lack of weapons, Zahir looked every inch the sheikh with his commanding presence. With guests such as these she knew it was imperative that he appeared a formidable king at all times. There must be no infringement on his dignity.

Suddenly she heard running feet.

With an impending sense of horror, she put her hand to her mouth, wanting to call out, to stop Matta from being rejected, to keep him from harm. He had no business to be there. But he was too far away. Neither Zahir, nor Matta, could see or hear her.

She watched as Matta bounded up to Zahir from behind and jump onto his leg, his little hands digging in to the folds of his robe. With one swift movement, Zahir had swept his arm around Matta's small body and swung him high in the air.

Appalled, Anna watched, waiting to see the inevitable. But it didn't come.

Matta's loud shrieks of joy echoed around the courtyard as Zahir swung him again and again into the air, catching him before he fell.

The guests laughed and turned away to leave.

As the adrenaline ebbed from her body, she sank against the wall for support. She felt sick and dazed. She continued to watch as Zahir swept the boy up until he sat across his shoulders, each leg firmly secured by Zahir's hands. As they turned toward the gardens, Anna caught sight of Matta's wide grin below eyes that shone bright in the sunlight.

By the time she reached them Matta was back on his feet, trying to catch up with his young cousins. She fell into step with Zahir as they made their way through to the rear entrance of the palace, out to a plateau that overlooked the wide plains.

She reached out and placed her hand lightly on his arm. He stopped walking immediately and turned to her expectantly.

"Zahir, I was wrong."

He raised an eyebrow. "I'm sure you were. But about what in particular?"

She even ignored his jibe. "About Matta."

"Ah." He nodded. She could see he understood.

"You were right. This is the place for him. He will be happy here."

He hesitated. For a moment she wondered if he realized what it had taken for her to say these words. Perhaps. Perhaps not. She would never know for he didn't speak. He simply nodded slowly.

"He *is* happy here. Look."

Her gaze followed his, out to where the boys were playing, safely within the battlements of the palace, safe from the plunging drop below, his nurse watching close by.

The late afternoon was giving way to a sunset that flooded the surrounding plain with fire, warming Zahir's face. She dropped her hand that was still touching his arm and stepped away.

"I have to go now."

"Get changed for dinner. We are not always so traditional. You are free to wear whichever of your clothes you like: traditional or western. You have plenty to choose from. I will send Matta in shortly."

She nodded. She couldn't even wait for her son. It was as if something inside her had shifted, the pressure was off. The wide-open plains, her son safe, she felt herself being lulled into a state she couldn't have imagined twenty-four hours previously. She needed to get away from Zahir. She needed time to think.

Zahir watched her go and smiled to himself. He wasn't sure exactly what it was that so reassured her. Presumably seeing the boy with his friends and relations. Whatever. The first part of his plan had gone well: reassure her about the child.

She was wrong. He hadn't underestimated her maternal instincts. The first stage of his plan of seduction was based on them. And, with that worry gone, she would know there was no other place for her than here. Now she had to realize that there was no other place for her than in his bed. And she would. She would soon see that there were worse things than being the wife and lover of Sheikh Zahir Al-Zaman of Qawaran.

∼

Dressed in one of the beautiful designer gowns that now filled her wardrobe, Anna looked through the east window, out to where a line of darkness crept over the plains as the fiery sun dipped behind the mountains. The view, so beguiling in its expanse, so different to the intimate beauty of the courtyard garden, called to her strongly. Her acceptance that Matta was where he needed to be came at a cost. The void she'd felt open within her, couldn't be filled. Part of her believed that that was enough; that was all she could hope for. But something deep inside demanded more. She closed her eyes and felt the wide, open space as though it were a living entity. Could she find her own freedom here?

The unearthly screech of a bird of prey echoed around the darkening plains and drew her attention up into the blood-red sky. She watched the huge falcon spread its tawny-black feathers and hover for a moment before swooping downwards suddenly. It flew past her window and landed on a man's outstretched gloved hand.

She could see the bird's plumage, rich and textured in the last of the fiery sun, could see it stretch its neck in pleasure as the man gently stroked the falcon's body. The falcon stopped pacing on the man's gloved hand, calmed and ducked his head in submission.

Then the bird let out a call, harsh and strong, as if it were a cry for freedom, a request to return to its previous state. A cry full of a longing for what it could no longer have. But it didn't move from the man's glove. The man might let it fly—give it its freedom when he chose—but, once his arm was outstretched he expected obedience; he expected the bird's return.

The man slid on the falcon's hood and moved into view. It was Zahir.

CHAPTER 3

She was late.

Zahir's gaze swept the table along which his extended family sat. They had already begun the banquet that was in her honor. Above the low hum of conversation and clatter of cutlery and glasses, Zahir could sense the atmosphere had become unsettled.

It was unheard of for a guest to be late. It was inexcusable. But then the woman seemed to have no idea how to behave or, if she did, went out of her way to do the opposite of what was expected.

He signaled for his glass to be re-filled and, rather than witness the frowns and puzzled looks of his family, focused on the subtle flicker of candlelight on the highly polished table.

His feelings toward Anna were as ambiguous as the shifting patterns of light on dark. There was no question that he wanted her for his wife and lover and that was his priority. But whether he could forgive her for betraying Abduallah by sleeping with him and for the lies that followed, he didn't know. Her behavior was anathema to him. And still the insults continued. Here, now, she was not only insulting his family but their tradition, their culture, their—

His train of thought was broken as the light that played on the darkly grained wood suddenly shimmered down its length. The flames of the candles sputtered and distorted as the door swung open silently. It was only when they had regained their steady glow that Zahir looked up. Anna was standing just inside the room: tall, elegant, and lost. All anger vanished as he felt his need for her slam hard deep inside. Blood roared in his ears, obliterating all else. There was only her.

The light caught the crystal beading on her dress, and reflected a silver glow into her eyes, making them appear almost spectral, just as he'd imagined they would. But he hadn't anticipated its effect on him. The gut-wrenching need was still there—always would be—but he felt a sense of her vulnerability, seeing her standing there so unsure. And for some reason it hurt.

He couldn't take his eyes off her as she walked toward the table—the gray silk dress shifting sensuously with each movement of her hips.

He rose to meet her, everyone else forgotten.

"Anna." He took her hand and pulled her to him. It was only when he saw her cast tentative smiles to the others that he turned from her, suddenly conscious of his family watching them. Understandably they were intensely curious about Abduallah's widow, of whom they knew so little.

"May I introduce Anna. Anna, my family."

"It's lovely to meet you at last." She flashed a wide, all-encompassing smile at everyone, her eyes connecting with individuals up and down the table in an intuitive intimacy that made each and every one believe her words were meant only for them. "And I'm so sorry I'm late. Matta was unsettled and wanted me to stay with him longer than usual."

All the women nodded with understanding and the men simply smiled admiringly: all irritation and any lingering doubts about this mysterious foreigner evaporating like water under the full force of the desert sun. It angered him, this ability of hers to charm people with a smile and a few words in her seductive low voice.

How did she get away with it, he wondered, as he introduced her to his cousins, aunts, uncles, and his sisters—Fatima who, with her children, lived at the palace, and Firyal, who was visiting from Paris? He seated Anna opposite him and watched as she continued to charm her family. She seemed to think she could do what she liked and all would be forgiven with a show of her charm. He turned abruptly to talk to his uncle unwilling to face the unsettling thought he, too, was not immune to her charm.

Anna knew she'd messed up big time; knew that Zahir wouldn't forgive her for such a breach of Bedu tradition. Hospitality was central to his culture and she'd just treated it as if it were of no importance. But Matta was her priority. She did as she had always done when confronted with failure —put on a big smile and acted like her mother, acted like nothing had happened. Trouble was, the bigger she acted, the smaller she felt.

She felt her smile quiver around her lips as she desperately tried to find the strength to face the intimidating al-Zaman clan.

Was Zahir going out of his way to intimidate her by presenting them all to her at once? Did he not realize how terrifying it was to be surrounded by the people who at best thought her family to be a bad influence on their younger brother, Abduallah and who, at worst, blamed her for his death and who now had to face the prospect of her marriage to their elder brother?

"Anna, it is so lovely to meet you at last." Fatima rose and kissed Anna's cheeks. "May I call you Anna?"

Anna's smile relaxed with relief at the warmth of Fatima's greeting.

"Of course."

"Not 'of course' at all. You are now my elder sister, despite the fact you are so much younger."

Anna raised her eyebrows in surprise.

"But you are a westerner, you do not know our ways. Did my brother—Abduallah, that is—not explain anything?"

"A little. He didn't talk much about his home, although I knew he missed it very much."

"And we missed him. We wanted him home, very much, but Zahir was unable to persuade him to return."

"No. He…" Anna trailed off instinctively wanting to talk with Fatima about Abduallah, tell her all the past that only she knew and that she desperately wanted to share with his family.

"There is no need to explain. Zahir said that Abduallah wouldn't return because he was happy where he was." Fatima shrugged. "Maybe, maybe not. All I know is that he was not like Zahir and Zahir did not understand him. But," she inclined her head, intimately toward her, "we women do. And Matta? I was surprised…" Her voice tailed off.

Anna looked at her warily, noting the curiosity in Fatima's eyes. So at least one member of Zahir's household suspected. Probably the only one, judging by the way she watched those around her.

"Well, it's complicated..."

Fatima touched her on the arm. "I did wonder and I mean no disrespect by my doubts. It was simply a feeling I had about Abduallah but it was obviously unfounded. I can see Matta is truly my nephew. But come, enough of this I am letting my tongue run away with me." Fatima nervously sipped her water, as if realizing that she'd gone too far.

Anna put out her hand on Fatima's and squeezed it. "It's OK. I'm not offended. I appreciate your honesty; I understand your doubts but you are right, Matta *is*, truly, your nephew."

"Yes, of course he is. I'm sorry, I didn't mean…"

"Forget it. Tell me about yourself. Why did you come back here? You were living in Riyadh were you not?"

"Yes. For ten years until my beloved husband died but he left little money and three children. Zahir insisted I return home."

"He seems to make a habit of that."

Fatima looked surprised at her implied criticism.

"Because he is sheikh; because he protects and cares for his family and people. My life has been far from easy and he has always looked after me, even if from a distance. You are in safe hands."

Anna searched the care-worn eyes and smiled, moved by the directness of this woman whose sadness was countered by a happy nature very different to her elder brother's.

"I am glad you are my sister. It's good not to feel alone."

Fatima looked shocked. "Alone? But you have your family in the United States, you had Abduallah and now you have Zahir." She laughed. "I cannot believe you feel alone."

"Believe me," Anna half-whispered turning to Fatima completely, "my family is not so numerous as yours, nor so close. And Zahir, well, he's a busy man."

"For you, no." Fatima bent her head to speak confidentially to Anna. "I have never known him stop working—until now. He was at war for much of his youth. And then when peace came, he had to ensure we became wealthy once more. It was just how it was. It's only now, with you, that I've ever known him to take time away from his business."

"I guess he wants to make sure I don't go anywhere."

"And where would you go? Why would you want to? No, he wants you. See how he looks at you."

Anna looked up and caught Zahir's gaze. His dark eyes were focused on her, watchful as always, but they held a different quality tonight. She tried, but couldn't look away. Perhaps it was the glow of the candles that gave his expression a seductive warmth. Or perhaps it was her own need for reassurance in these alien surroundings among strangers. Whichever, his gaze, while still heated, didn't sear tonight but rather enveloped, wrapped around and held her like the warmth of a desert breeze once evening had fallen.

The gentle touch of Fatima's hand on hers broke the spell.

"You see? You have nothing to fear about loneliness, ever again."

Anna was shocked at Fatima's words. It had been her need to break the connection with her family that had driven her hard for independence and freedom. But now, the tentacles of family and relationships were slowly winding their intrusive bonds around her, drawing her closer to them. She sipped the iced water, relishing its chill effect down her body, trying to calm the rising panic.

Was there no way out of this palace that was a fortress; was there no escape from this family whose sense of loyalty and duty bound them together; was there no avoiding this man who called to her as surely as he called to his falcon, demanding capture?

"I hope you will allow me to help you in the coming week, in the lead up to the wedding."

"Wedding." Anna repeated softly, feeling the iron doors close with a clang behind her. Her mind turned to the way the falcon had shivered with excitement at Zahir's touch, accepting his command.

"Zahir has organized it of course but I would be happy to

help you personally to prepare, if I may? You only have four days now."

"Four days?"

"I'm sorry, you did not know?" Fatima looked anxiously over at Zahir. "Oh dear. He will not like that I've told you then."

"Well it's good someone has."

By the way Fatima was looking at Zahir she could see that Zahir was accustomed to his family doing everything he said, obeying his every wish, anticipating his every demand. No wonder he thought he could do the same to her. Well that was one tradition she could definitely do without.

"An oversight, I'm sure. But there is no need to be anxious, all will be ready on time. Zahir instructed preparations to begin a month ago. Ample time to have everything arranged. He is so organized."

Organized wasn't the word that sprang to Anna's mind. He'd only proposed yesterday. She'd only said "yes" yesterday. But he'd organized the wedding weeks ago. He'd been so sure.

"Zahir controls everything around here doesn't he?"

Fatima shrugged. "Of course. As I say, he is the sheikh. So, tomorrow, I will wait upon you, as tradition holds."

"And we do everything by tradition?"

"Naturally. It is tradition for a reason—because it works." She smiled sympathetically. "You will become accustomed to our ways soon. Everyone does things by the ways of their country."

Anna shook her head. "Not me. I do things my way."

Fatima shook her head gently. "Not anymore, Anna. Now it is *our* way. Don't fight it. It is a good tradition you are following after all. You are marrying your dead husband's brother. That is good. It helps strengthen the family ties. I just wish my poor husband had an available brother. But still, I am here with Zahir, with my family. And he is a good man."

A good man. The words rang in her head. They seemed so far from the truth. He was a hard man, a controlling man—a warrior living in a civilized world. He was a magnetic man. But good?

The rest of the evening flowed by in a stream of small-talk and pleasantries. All Anna's fears of rejection and mistrust evaporated before the genuine interest and warmth of Zahir's family. By the time coffee was served, Anna discovered to her surprise that she'd actually enjoyed herself. Discovering more about the al-Zaman family, she'd come to understand a little more about Abduallah —and Zahir.

Suddenly Anna was aware that a quiet had descended. She looked up to find Zahir had risen and stood facing her.

"Come, Anna. We must leave. We have business to attend."

"Now?"

He smiled tightly. "Yes, otherwise I would not have mentioned it."

She smiled at Fatima and, bidding the others goodnight, followed Zahir out of the room and into the corridor along which the flames of huge torches flickered, sending shafts of light into its lofty heights.

"Business? What business?"

"You will see. It will give us time to talk also."

"You haven't exactly appeared over-eager to talk to me so far."

"I think you can reasonably assume that I'm angry."

"And I think I can reasonably assume that you're always angry."

"No. Only when people are unforgivably rude. You were late. It is unforgivable to be late."

"Matta was over-tired. I needed to be with him to settle him down."

"That is what Muma Yemena is there for."

"He wanted me."

"You needed to be here. To do your duty."

"My duty is to my son."

"Your son needs to toughen up. You will be my wife now. Your duties are wide-ranging: they are to the family above all, they are to respect our culture, our ways, me."

"You'll have to forgive me." She couldn't help a sarcastic tone creeping in. "My ways are different to yours. I have no sense of duty to my family."

He stopped and opened a door. "No. Of course you haven't."

Anna stepped inside the library, filled floor to ceiling with books. Above them a mezzanine floor made the most of the high ceiling by providing another layer of book shelves. It smelt of old books, leather, and strong coffee. Apart from the books the room was dominated by a large leather-topped desk, in front of which Zahir pulled out a seat for Anna.

She sat down but she didn't wait for him to take control.

"I understand we are to be married at the end of this week."

"Yes."

"Were you going to bother telling me?"

"Of course. It is not a subject for idle chatter, although my sister obviously believes so. It is business. And that is why I wished to meet with you now. To complete the paperwork."

"Marriage equals paperwork. Interesting."

"No more unusual than your own marriage."

"At least I played an active part in that."

"Here. You need to sign these."

"What are they?" She didn't bring them to her nor attempt to read them.

"A pre-nuptial. If you leave without my agreement within five years, Matta will remain with me and you will forfeit the funds I intend to gift you."

"And that's traditional Bedu culture is it?"

His eyes glittered. "No. In traditional Bedu culture the woman becomes a property of the man. But we no longer live in the Dark Ages—"

"Could have fooled me. I thought that was what you wanted—to own me, to do what you wanted with me." Her breath quickened.

"I have no interest in a one-way transaction. That will give me no satisfaction. I want you willing; I wish to enjoy your enjoyment."

A memory flashed into her mind: of his fingers touching her lips as they sucked in ragged breaths, of his eyes watching her face intently as she climaxed and of how, only then, did he come to his own intense climax. She breathed in sharply and willed herself to focus.

"Transactions, business. This is what it all comes down to with you isn't it?"

"Yes. Never think it is anything else."

"I wouldn't. I doubt you've an ounce of genuine feeling or affection in you."

He gazed coolly at her for one long moment before continuing. "Why do you fight this, Anna? Here, take the papers and sign."

"I'll read them first."

"Then do so." He rose and walked over to an intricately carved cabinet. On top of it was a small stove heating a coffee pot. Two small cups sat beside it.

"Coffee?"

"No thanks."

She leaned over the desk, one hand propping her chin as

she read through the papers and tried to ignore the fact that Zahir was two feet away from her and watching her closely.

She didn't have to concentrate hard; the papers were as familiar to her as a daily newspaper. Even from her incomplete law studies at Cornell she knew that he'd been more than fair to her in the pre-nuptial agreement. She'd entered this marriage with no assets and, if she divorced him after five years, she'd leave an extremely wealthy woman.

But she didn't care about wealth. Could she sign her life away? But it wasn't about *her* life was it? It was about Matta. In the past twenty-four hours she'd discovered that Matta was home. That this was the best place for him to grow up into the man she knew he could become. She'd been worried about Zahir's harsh influence. But even that view had changed since she'd seen Zahir in his own environment with the people around him who cared and respected and admired him. And the way he was with Matta.

A vision of Matta's joyous face, as Zahir had swooped him up and placed him on his shoulders, would be imprinted in her memory forever, made all the more vivid by the acute fears that had preceded it.

She had to do her best for her son and if that meant signing her life away in order to be able to watch him grow up, then so be it.

She signed and pushed the papers away from her.

"No questions?"

"I know these documents, I studied them, I know the implications. I've already agreed to them in spirit. There, now you have it in black and white." She rose from her chair. "So if that's all, I'll go to bed."

"No. Not quite all. You haven't read the other set of papers."

She looked down in surprise. She'd assumed they were

nothing to do with her. She'd assumed the only thing Zahir wanted was the pre-nuptial agreement. And he'd got that.

She didn't move but narrowed her eyes and looked up at him suspiciously.

"What are these about?"

"Read them and see."

She flicked them open and read.

Wide eyed she simply stared at him. Her heart thudded and she could feel the heat of excitement flood her body. Her hand trembled as she folded them lengthwise again and sat down, unable to believe what she'd just read, unable to say a word.

"I'm sorry. I thought that this would be something you would want."

He'd mistaken her lack of speech for displeasure. But still she couldn't trust herself to speak.

"You don't wish to complete your legal studies at Riyadh and Paris?" he continued.

"Of course I do." She wouldn't have recognized her voice if she hadn't felt her breath against her lips.

"Then why do you look as if I've just struck you?"

"Because you have." How could she convey her absolute shock at his offer for her to complete her law degree? The arrangements he'd made to have her come to Qarawan had all been on his terms, as had his taking of Matta from her, his anger with her, his desire for her—all had been on his terms. Now this.

This was for her.

"To appease your conscience?"

"I have nothing to appease my conscience about. I have done the best for everyone in getting you and Matta here. It is how our society operates. I had to do whatever it took to bring you both home."

"And this is what you want?"

"Of course. I want you. I've been clear about that all along. But I want you to know that your life doesn't end here. It goes on—with me. It goes on—with Matta. It goes on—with your studies."

She looked down at the papers once more, not trusting herself to look into his eyes. Tears pressed against her lids. She shook her head. He came and stood beside her. She could feel his strength like a drug. All she had to do was reach out and take it. It would make her feel whole again. Something she hadn't felt since she'd last slept with him. She wanted him to touch her. She willed him to touch her.

But he didn't. He was so close that she could feel the heat from his body. She could see his hands flex, as if to control their movement—his skin rich and warm and tantalizing.

Whether he knew it or not, he'd reached the only part of her that was still vulnerable—the hopes and dreams ingrained in her since childhood. He'd reached that vulnerable part and broken down all the other defenses that she'd built against a direct line of attack upon her. She'd never anticipated that he'd do such a thing.

"Take the papers. They have all the information you need. I have arranged for you to study by correspondence. But you will also need to travel."

"But Matta?"

"He may come with you, visit you if you are to be away for a while. But it hardly seems sensible if you will be focusing on your studies. He may as well be here with his family."

She nodded and looked back down at the papers.

"You won't need to attend the university in person immediately. Matta will be settled by then."

"He seems pretty settled already."

"Of course."

"And that's down to you. You've made him feel welcome, at home here. Thank you."

"He is of my blood. This will always be his home. No need to thank me."

"And thank you for this. It's the first time that, well…"

He touched her hair and she closed her eyes as his fingertips slid smoothly down the length of her hair, like a gift of all she could desire.

"You have nothing to thank me for. It is you who will do all the work."

"But you thought of me." How could she tell him that no one had ever respected her thirst for education, her need for independence, her hopes and dreams before.

He took her hand and pulled it to his lips.

He frowned. "And this is unusual?"

"You must know it is."

"But your own family, Anna, they may have been dysfunctional but surely they cared for you?"

"Possibly. But they cared for their own brand of escape more."

He considered for a moment. Frowned. "You were strong, then, not to choose the path of your mother and your brother."

"Strong? No. Just different. Their lives scared me. And I was good at school. I had choices."

"Everyone has choices."

"No. *They* didn't."

His hands caressed her arms lightly. She could feel his breath on her skin; she could smell coffee and the earthy scent of his aftershave, a blend of leather and amber, creating a heady mix that made her feel dizzy with longing. He leaned forward. She closed her eyes, her mouth softening readying for the press of his lips against hers. Instead she felt his lips upon her forehead. The kiss was gentle and his lips lingered on her face for one long moment, long enough for her to want more. Then he drew away.

"Come. It is time for bed."

As if in a dream she felt his hand lightly draw her to him as they left the library, heading back to their private quarters. Moonlight flooded the corridors, slanting its beams across the passageways, revealing a gentle magic to the imposing palace, a seductive magic.

They walked in silence until they reached the courtyard garden that divided their rooms. The gentle sound of water splashing in the fountain broke the heavy stillness of the night. The white blossom of the jasmine and orange trees appeared almost luminescent under an indigo sky filled with the brilliance of a new moon and innumerable stars. Anna had never seen so many. It seemed in the darkness of the desert that light, of any kind, shone more brightly. She looked up into his eyes whose own darkness was now rimmed with the same silver light.

"I can't be bought, Zahir."

"I have no wish to purchase you. I wish to make you happy."

She sucked in her breath sharply, turned away and entered her room alone. She would not cry in front of him.

CHAPTER 4

Through the open window Zahir watched the curtains to Anna's room sway in the cool night breeze, across the courtyard.

Happy? Did he really want to make her happy? He wanted her in his home, yes; wanted her in his bed, yes. But happy?

He moved away abruptly and opened the western window that looked out over the hammada plains and took a deep breath. Sometimes he longed for the open spaces and air of the desert, where the only dictates were ones of survival.

Life had been simple then.

He pressed both hands onto the wall either side of the window and closed his eyes tightly.

From what deep instinct had those words surfaced? He shook his head. He didn't even want to know. He refused to know. The only reason he wanted her happy was because he wished to seduce her. Pure and simple.

He undressed quickly and got into bed, determined to rid himself of the uncontrollable thoughts that haunted him. He needed the chaos to end. He willed his body and mind into the old numbing pattern that had enabled him to control not only himself but others, that had kept him and his men alive during ten years of desert warfare. And that he needed now, more than ever.

∼

SHE WOULD HAVE to tell him.

She brushed her hair vigorously until it shone in the morning light and then stopped suddenly, arrested by the look of apprehension in her eyes.

But how do you tell a man that the child he believes to be his nephew is, in fact, his own child?

She took a deep breath and continued to brush her hair.

God knows. But she'd have to find a way. She'd intended never to tell Zahir that Matta was his own son. For years she'd worried that he would take Matta away from her. But now the worst had happened and it turned out that it wasn't the worst thing that could have happened. Maybe, for Matta, it was the best.

Whatever else she might think of Zahir, he had given her son a home and a family like none she could have given him. And not only that, he'd given her the gift of completing her education: a gift she hadn't imagined in a million years.

He deserved to know. And he also needed to know another fact of which he was very obviously unaware—that Matta couldn't have been Abduallah's son because she'd never lain with Abduallah, that Abduallah had no interest in her in that way because she was the wrong sex.

Suddenly she felt his presence. She turned sharply to see him silhouetted against the already bright sunlight.

"Zahir! Haven't you heard of knocking?"

"The doors were open. I imagined that you would have closed them if you wished for privacy."

"Privacy? What's that? I have a child, remember. I keep my door open for him. Not that it would matter, he'd come in anyway."

"Your western ways are very strange to me. We will need privacy when we are married."

She blushed as her mind followed the drift of his thoughts. "Really?" She looked him firmly in the eye.

"When we make love."

His eyes caressed her as surely as if his fingers touched her lips and his hands traced the curves of her body. She took a deep breath.

"Remember, that's not part of the agreement."

"It doesn't need to be." His eyes held both reassurance and heat: a delicate balance that stopped her from running but didn't stop her from wanting. She swallowed.

"Turn around, Anna."

She narrowed her eyes, not trusting him. "I promise not to lay you on the bed and take you here and now. Not yet, anyway." It was all she could do to suppress the tiny intake of breath that his words provoked. She couldn't move. Instead he moved around behind her.

"Hey, what are you up to?"

"Stay still." He lifted her hair gently and dropped a cool necklace around her throat. "I wanted to give you these by way of apology."

"You, apologize?"

"I should have told you about the wedding before you learned about it from my sister."

"Yes you should. But there are so many things you should have done that I'm surprised you've chosen only this one to apologize for."

"It is only this that I regret." He finished clipping the necklace in place. "It was my mother's, of course, and now yours."

She fingered the chunky stones and lifted it to see a thick strand of emeralds and diamonds shoot light onto the walls and ceiling as she turned it in her hands.

"My God. It's beautiful." She looked into his eyes. "Are you sure? Do you really want me to have this?"

"We are getting married, Anna. It should be yours. I want you to have it."

She was acutely aware of his chest so close to her back that the impulse to rest against its strength was near impossible to resist. But she did resist. She focused on the necklace in the mirror, and then glanced at him from under lowered lashes. His eyes glowed too, perhaps a reflection from the necklace.

"Thank you. It's beautiful."

"*You* are beautiful." He frowned slightly and almost absently hooked a thick strand of hair away from her necklace, as if to admire the necklace better. "But you need to hurry. Fatima will be waiting for you. And I will be leaving for a few days, as tradition demands."

She sighed. "Yes, I know. Fatima told me. I'm nearly ready."

She scooped her hair up into a French twist and struggled to contain it within the antique ivory comb that she'd found on her dressing table.

"Here let me help."

With a practiced twist he swept her hair up and caught it with the comb.

"Where did you learn that trick?"

"The comb also belonged to my mother. I used to watch her get ready, help her sometimes."

"Your mother?" She turned to stare at him. "I thought you hardly remembered her?"

There was a long silence. "One remembers moments,

fragments of memories." He opened the door and stood to one side. "Fatima will be waiting for you."

They walked down the sun-streaked corridor in silence for a few moments as Anna absorbed the images that raced through her mind: of a boy who so intently watched a beloved mother do her hair that he could replicate the same twist and tuck two decades later, of a boy who lost her when he was far too young.

"Please, tell me more about your mother. Abduallah never talked about her."

"He was too young. He never knew her and Mother never knew him."

"She would have liked him as well as loved him."

"Of course. We all did. He would have had a great life if only he had not surrounded himself with negative influences."

She stopped abruptly at the entrance to the library. "We have to talk. You blame me, but you don't know the full story."

"I know the end of the story. He died. That is enough."

"No, really, there are some things you need to know."

He shook his head. "No. There are some things *you* need to know. Abduallah wasn't just my brother, he embodied all that I was fighting for. Those years spent half-starving in the desert, blood on my hands, and blood in my heart, it was his image that I held in my mind; it was the only thing that kept me sane. Everything I did I did so that *he* could be free to lead a good Bedu life. Nothing could sully that image. Nothing. So don't try."

"I wouldn't, I couldn't, sully his image. But he was a man with problems—"

"His only problem was that he left Qawaran and met people who took advantage of him."

"People like me I suppose you mean."

He closed his eyes briefly and sighed.

"No. I don't believe you took advantage of him. I believe you genuinely cared for him but it was the influence of others that led to his death."

"I'm sorry. But—"

He placed his hand on her lips. "Anna, please, leave me my memories of him."

Slowly she nodded her head. He brought her hand to his lips and kissed it. He knew something—perhaps only a little—but he knew enough to know that he didn't want to know anymore.

"I must go now but I will see you when I return, the night before the ceremony."

She felt a flutter of nerves and he narrowed his eyes.

"You know what to do at the ceremony?"

She nodded. "I've been over it with Fatima. It's just that there are so many people here, so much expected of me."

"When you enter the room, just look at me."

She smiled. "And wouldn't you just like that?"

He smiled a secret smile, turned and walked away, his soft leather-clad footsteps the only sound in the echoing hall.

She watched him leave, aware for the first time that this strong man had an inner vulnerability that he had carefully encased in stone. He was doing his best to ensure that nothing got through to it. If Abduallah had embodied Zahir's hope for the future, what would it do to Zahir to know that Abduallah had been careening headlong down a path to self-destruction long before he met Anna? What would he do if he knew that the very traditions that Zahir held dear had destroyed Abduallah? As a gay man—albeit a celibate one—Abduallah believed, rightly or wrongly, that he could never live up to his family's and culture's expectations of him and he'd hated himself for it. The hate had eaten away at him until he'd wanted to destroy his body, just as surely as his soul was being eaten away. And there had been nothing Anna could do to help her best friend.

No, she'd not tell Zahir. He would continue to despise her for her apparent disloyalty to Abduallah and for the lies she'd told to keep his secret, but she could bear it for the sake of Abduallah and the memories of her friend that lay deep within the heart of his family.

∽

From her vantage point, tucked in a cave carved out of the sandstone escarpment high above the palace by one of the many springs, Anna watched Zahir's convoy of four-wheel drives bump across the desert returning toward the palace.

For three days and three nights Zahir had been absent, out in the desert with his people. But now he was returning. She realized with sudden clarity that she'd missed him. He was so strong she wanted to cling to him; he was so inwardly vulnerable she wanted to fight for him; he was so infuriating she wanted to scream at him. He was everything that was contradictory and she'd missed him.

She wanted desperately to see him but knew it unlikely. He'd be busy. She closed her eyes and remembered how he looked at her, with the heat and intensity she'd become used to. At first it had been too fierce. But it had gentled, she realized, just as her own bitterness had faded. The heat was still left but all the destructive emotions had fallen away.

She took the necklace from her bag and held it up to the light that split into rainbows as it passed through the multifaceted stones. She closed her eyes. But even then, closing her eyes, closing her heart, against such light, failed to stop it from entering. What point was there in denying it then?

Zahir stopped on the threshold of the cave and looked down at Anna. Her lips were curved into a faint smile as if dreaming of something wonderful. Her face was lightly flushed, the soft sprinkle of freckles across the bridge of her nose made her look ridiculously young. She looked well, better than when she'd arrived. The good food and rest had nourished her. He watched as her eyelids flickered lightly and drifted open.

"What were you dreaming of? You looked so peaceful."

"Thinking I'm dreaming of you, Zahir?" Her tone was gently teasing.

"No. I don't wish to inspire such peace."

She laughed. "And you don't. Believe me." She smiled up to him. "Come, lie here and I will tell you what I was dreaming of."

He raised his eyebrows but to his own surprise found himself lying on his side, facing her.

"So obedient." A smiled played on her lips.

"Only because it allows me to watch you more closely."

"Close your eyes."

"Now that I will not do."

She sighed. "OK then, just listen. What do you hear?"

"Water."

"Exactly. I was dreaming of rain. Not the thunderous sort, but really soft, gentle rain. The sort of rain that is scarcely stronger than mist but can penetrate hard-packed earth. That's the kind of rain I was imagining."

"We get rain here."

"Yeah, right. When?"

"Soon. The rains will come soon. And then you will see miracles happen."

They were only a foot away from each other, but neither came any closer.

"Miracles. Do they happen? I don't think so."

"Then you know very little. Miracles happen if you open your eyes and see."

The humor fell away from her expression as she searched his eyes. "My eyes are open now."

"And what do you see."

"You."

"And am I not a miracle?"

She raised an eyebrow. "In a way, yes. It's a miracle that just one person can contain such conceit."

"No." His expression remained serious. "I mean it, Anna. You've performed a miracle on me. Without me knowing how you've done it, you've robbed me of my anger. *That*, is a miracle."

"And what has replaced your anger?"

He reached out his hand and gently touched her cheek with the tip of his index finger.

Anna closed her eyes involuntarily at his touch. It was the merest of brushes but it held the strength of a match lighting her skin and body with fire.

She pressed her eyes more firmly closed as his finger whispered a caress, tracing the line of her cheekbone and round beneath her ear, before the back of his fingers brushed lightly beneath her jaw. Time seemed to have slowed, allowing her mind and body to register each tiny movement against her skin. Physically it was as soft as a puff of warm wind against warm skin: no contrasts, scarcely any contact. But sensually his touch was like the caress of fire on ice that had kept itself frozen for too long.

It was only when she no longer felt the heat of his touch that she could gather enough control over her emotions to open her eyes. She didn't want him to see what she was feeling. Not yet.

What she saw when she opened her eyes was an unexpected tenderness in those exquisitely lashed dark, dark eyes.

"Tell me Anna, why won't you let me make love to you?"

She didn't reply immediately. Answers formed in her mind: bright, quick, facile ones that had always been part of her mask and sharp, defensive ones that she'd turned to when she'd felt her mask slipping. But neither could help her now. Only the truth.

"You know why."

He shook his head. "No. Tell me."

"You've made my life hell since Abduallah died."

"That was then. This is now. I believe I have ceased to make your life hell."

"Because you have what you want."

He nodded. "That is so. So tell me, do you still hate me?"

She frowned. "You took my son without my permission, you've blackmailed me into marrying you. What do you think?"

"I don't know. That is why I am asking. I am hoping that you realize why I did these things now. Do you still hate me?"

How could she, looking into his eyes? No, she felt no hatred, only desire. But still she couldn't say it, couldn't admit that all he had predicted was coming to pass.

"I, I can't think of that now."

She moved away, desperate to place some distance between them—physical and emotional. He stood up first and pulled her to standing beside him.

"Then when?"

"Isn't it enough that I'm marrying you? Tomorrow I'm going to be paraded before your people like some trophy and that, I am not looking forward to."

"If it is any comfort most of it is for our people. We have the starring role but only for a little while. The rest of the time is for them."

She nodded and looked out over the plains.

He reached over and took her hand. His thumb rubbed down the length of the back of her hand.

"I want to hate you." Her voice was low. She didn't pull her hand away.

"But you don't."

She shook her head.

"So what's changed?"

"You. Understanding you."

"Good. Come here."

"No. I am seeing Matta now, he's been practicing a dance for him and his cousins to perform at the wedding." She tried to pull away awkwardly. "I must go. Now."

He smiled and continued to hold her hand; his grip was gentle but firm.

"Matta is fitting in very well." Zahir turned her hand in his, studying it with an appreciation that sent shivers down her whole body. "His language, his behavior, one would never know that he hadn't been born in Qarawan."

"He's done well. I'm so proud."

"You have brought him up well. You have given him the foundation upon which he can step forward into what must have seemed a strange culture to him."

"I gave him love, that was all I could do."

"That was obviously enough."

She closed her eyes as his hand brushed the back of hers in a fleeting caress that sent shivers of excitement down her arm.

"Zahir, I must go." But she made no move to leave, transfixed by the look on his face.

Slowly he pulled her to him and kissed her on the lips. It was as gentle as his touch and as shocking. There was nothing insistent about his kiss. His lips brushed hers before opening gently and caressing hers. It was like no other kiss she'd ever had. Her whole being was concentrated in that one touch. And her whole being was devastated as the touch withdrew.

"Now, go, see to my nephew."

Anna stepped away as if forced back by his words. He was wooing her and it was working. But it was all based on an untruth—one she couldn't continue to live with.

CHAPTER 5

Fatima stood back and appraised Anna's reflection in the mirror critically. "No. We need more foundation. Anna! You Americans are so pale!"

"Enough!" Anna brought her hands to her face and rose from the chair around which the women clustered. She couldn't take it anymore. Three hours of fussing and she looked like an orange-tinted Barbie doll.

Fatima exchanged looks with the others and dismissed them from the room.

"What is wrong, Anna?"

Anna stared at herself in the mirror. "Look at me. I don't even look like me." She picked up a wad of cotton wool and began wiping the heavy make-up off her face.

"It's tradition, it's—"

"Everything's tradition. I'm sick of your traditions. Fatima! It's not me. I'm sorry, I know you've been working hard but I've had enough."

It was Fatima's turn to be angry. "Then you should have said something before instead of sitting there like some kind of frozen mannequin."

"I know. I'm sorry, I'm sorry, I'm sorry."

"Saying it three times won't make it any better."

Anna looked up into Fatima's eyes, reflected back at her in the mirror, and realized that she'd really hurt her. She groped for her hand behind her. "I'm your younger sister, right? And sometimes younger sisters can be stupid."

"You are my elder sister, don't forget. Which, according to your logic, makes me the stupid one." Fatima squeezed Anna's hand. "Now tell me what this is really about." Fatima drew up a seat beside Anna.

Anna rested her elbows on the dressing table in front of the mirror and rubbed the heels of her palms into her eyes, smudging the black make-up all around her eyes.

"I can't help thinking of Abduallah."

"Ah." Fatima sat down as if all had been explained. "Abduallah. He was such a fun boy, always getting up to mischief and so beautiful."

Anna's eyes dropped. "Not so beautiful at the end." She was going to continue until she saw Fatima's hurt frown. "Look, I'm sorry. You're right. I'm being silly. Perhaps I just need a little time to myself."

Fatima nodded, her thoughts obviously still lingering over Anna's words. "You have five minutes and then we will return."

Anna smiled. "Just five minutes and then I promise I'll behave, but no foundation."

Fatima shrugged. "You want to look as pale as a lily on your wedding day, that's up to you."

Anna nodded. "It is."

Fatima's smile was different to most people's, Anna thought. It started in the eyes and spread down her rounded cheeks and made her lips curl last of all. It was like Zahir's, except that Zahir's smile stayed in his eyes and went nowhere else. He'd spent too long keeping an impassive face to the world to allow the sweet lip curl that Fatima displayed.

As the door closed quietly shut, Anna slipped to the cool floor and leaned against the wall. She closed her eyes and let the memories that wouldn't stay put, wouldn't do as they were told, flood her mind.

Memories of Abduallah, the last time she'd seen him, as he'd drifted into a stupor from which he couldn't be roused. If Fatima thought she looked pale, then she wouldn't have recognized Abduallah. His skin had turned a gray parchment color and had sunk dryly into his skull. She couldn't even remember his eyes because he always kept them closed to her. Closed to life.

She forced herself to remember the real Abduallah, the one she'd met at a party, so charming and kind, so handsome and, she'd thought, so honest. It was only after the brief registry office wedding that he'd told her the truth—that he needed Anna to show to his family that he was straight. Except he wasn't.

She'd swiftly organized a divorce but her affection for him hadn't faded and she agreed to present a united front to meet his brother. And afterwards, when Abduallah had seen the baby, he'd never asked her who the father was—although she suspected he knew—and he had been thrilled, adored the boy.

But not enough to stop the slow downward spiral. She'd tried to save him, to tell him not to give up, that there was a life for him. But the image of his unforgiving world was deeply ingrained and he did give up.

And that was the image before her now: his face, ravaged by drugs and despair. And it was not one she was able to share with his family.

She hadn't noticed Fatima enter until she felt her light touch on her shoulder.

"Don't cry, Anna. It will be all right. Abduallah wouldn't want you to be unhappy."

Anna shakily brought her hand up to her eyes, trying to hide her grief from Fatima. She'd kept it hidden for so long, tied up tight within her so that Matta wouldn't see, so that no one would see. But Fatima pulled Anna's hand down. "Don't hide from me, Anna. Your sadness is my sadness. We are family."

But for some reason that made Anna cry more. Fatima knelt down to face Anna and drew her to her, bringing her arms around her and let Anna sob into her shoulder.

After a few minutes, when the sobbing had subsided, Fatima pushed Anna away and looked at her critically. She pulled her to standing and sat her in front of the mirror.

Anna smiled—a watery kind of smile—at Fatima.

"Thank you."

"So you should," Fatima joked as she opened the door for the others to re-enter. "Ladies," she sighed heavily and theatrically. "I'm afraid we'll have to start again."

∽

Anna had been inside the palace mosque before but not when it was full of people dressed in their most extravagant clothes and jewels, not when all the attention was focused on one person: her.

She looked up, above the people and forest-like complexity of pillars, and fixed her gaze on the multitude of ornate lamps and candles under which the room seemed to shimmer with an unsteady light.

From under the slight protection of the filmy lace veil, Anna searched for Zahir and found him. His eyes, like those of everyone else, were focused on her, just like he said they'd be. The roomful of people seemed to fade under the shimmering light and there was only her and Zahir, only one way to go—an effect that was reinforced by the herringbone pattern inlaid on the stone floor that led her to him.

She became aware then, of the drag of the long, ornate train that fell behind her; the stiffness of the crystal-encrusted bodice that sparkled under the shifting lights and the glow and shimmer of the pale gray satin and lace veil.

Slowly the murmurs of the hundreds of people assembled in the mosque and the soaring music faded from her ears. She simply focused on him, almost communicated across the open space with him. It was the only way she'd get through this. He was also dressed in exquisite robes, his eyes lighter than she'd seen them, a smile softly hovering on his lips. Almost, she thought, as if he were happy.

He took her hand when she reached him and they sat side by side on ornately gilded chairs.

"You look beautiful." He whispered into her ear. But it was the squeeze of his hand from which she derived the most comfort. She took a deep breath and allowed the world back in again.

He continued to hold her hand as he turned to the assembled people and nodded. One simple nod, Anna thought, was enough to start proceedings. Person after person came up to them with gifts and speeches, paying homage to their sheikh and celebrating with him his long-awaited marriage. Despite Zahir's reassurances, she felt like a fraud. None of these people knew that the marriage was a sham and would be over once Zahir had had enough of her.

The mosque descended into respectful silence as the imam delivered his speech. Anna could make out only a little of it but knew that it was about honor and that he was calling on Zahir to heed his words. Zahir dipped his head in dignified agreement. The imam turned to Anna and, standing in place of the father she never knew, gave her hand to Zahir.

Two elder Bedu signed the marriage contract and it was only when the crowd collectively cheered that Anna knew that she was married—for the second time.

It was a farce. It was all she could think as congratulatory shouts rang through the air. The whole thing was a farce. She was here for as long as it took Zahir to tire of her. And that was the truth.

She felt something drain from her then.

Zahir inclined his head and whispered in her ear.

"Keep strong, Anna. We are married now. We only have a reception and then you will be free."

She closed her eyes briefly at the irony of his words.

He offered his hand to her. "Come."

The time for hesitation had gone and she took his hand. He led her through the mosque, the crowds of people following them in a procession that led to the reception room. Here they once more sat on two chairs raised above the others, as if they were royalty which, she realized, she was now.

One ceremony merged into another. The toasts, the swapping of the rings from the right to left index fingers, the speeches, the dances, the tributes; she remained smiling through it all and remembered Abduallah. He should have been here and he would have been if he hadn't believed that the very culture that he loved so much would reject him if it knew the truth about him. She couldn't help believe that he was wrong and that such a warm and vibrant culture with a reputation for hospitality and kindness would be inclusive and welcoming of everyone—especially one of their most vulnerable people, especially Abduallah.

IT WAS LATE into the evening before Zahir bent to her and spoke loudly over the music.

"We can go now. It is expected."

He rose and everyone stopped what they were doing and bowed.

Zahir had been watching her all day and knew there was something happening behind the polite, smiling façade. He could see it in her eyes. But he said nothing. There was time for that later.

Zahir took her hand and led her away, the music from the stringed instruments following them eerily through the flame-lit corridors to his suite of rooms.

She halted, momentarily, before she entered the room. He felt her hesitancy, her unease.

He followed her gaze as she looked around his room, trying to see it through her eyes. She'd not been there before. It was larger than her own and, while not as luxuriously detailed, it was just as sensuous with the richly-woven rugs on the stone floor, the silk curtains that shivered in the warm breeze and the soft scent of jasmine that filled the air.

Conscious of every nuance of her mood and emotion he heard her exhale the stress of the wedding and she revealed in a quick glance that she had shed the public image she'd been showing all day. This was the Anna only he knew: sensitive, vulnerable, and warm. But she was also tired. His fingers involuntarily stroked the darkened shadows under eyes. He wanted to kiss her, to hold her, to make love to her but he couldn't. She wasn't ready yet.

"You look very tired. Your face is strained."

"Not surprising. I feel like I've been on a stage, playing the role of my life, for the last eight hours."

"Don't tell me you're not used to acting. I've seen you assume a role, I've seen you act a part. At dinner that first night."

"Sometimes it's necessary to pretend"—she shrugged—"to hide myself."

"No more. Don't pretend any more with me, Anna. Come." He touched her face, closed his eyes at the silkiness of her skin and let his finger trail down to her jaw line where he traced it to her ear. She was truly exquisite. He sighed and drew her to a seat.

He sat opposite her to admire her beauty.

"Why no more pretense, Zahir? Aren't I still acting? Don't pretend this is a real marriage because it isn't. You've always made that very clear."

"I want it to be as real as it can be. The imam spoke of the need to honor each other and I believe in that. I will do that. But for honor we need truth."

Anna sighed. "The truth. I want to tell you the truth but I don't think you want to listen."

"Ridiculous, of course I do."

"About Abduallah?"

He shifted in his seat, brushed off a speck of imaginary dust. "Abduallah? I know the truth of Abduallah. He was my brother."

"Zahir, you were away for much of the time when he was growing up."

He rose abruptly and walked to the window that overlooked the plains, seeking reassurance from the dark emptiness that surrounded them, just as he had learned to gain strength from the desert as a boy at war. Slowly he turned to face her. "Anna, he was my brother and I knew him. He was all that was good about my family, about my people—full of life and charm."

"Not toward the end he wasn't. Yes, he was charming. He had a kind and gentle heart, but it wasn't one that was at ease with the world."

He gripped the rounded stone of the wall that surrounded the window. "No," he shook his head. "You are wrong."

She had to be wrong. He felt her hand on his shoulder,

tentative at first, as if she wasn't sure if she should. But then she gripped him with an urgency, a sureness of purpose that made him realize she believed what she was saying and was trying to convince him. He didn't turn around. She had to be wrong.

"I don't think I am wrong, Zahir. I'm sorry, but there were two Abduallahs—the laughing, charming, warm, and funny one—and the—"

"No!"

"And the one who couldn't find his way in the world."

He turned to her then, his own hand clasping hers, keeping it pressed firmly against his body.

He knew Abduallah. Anna didn't.

"Don't tell me about him. Tell me about you and him. Tell me why you married him." He rose and took her hand. "Come outside and tell me."

The dark night was what he needed after so much light and noise. The peace of the desert. There was no moon now, nothing to dim the brilliance of the stars overhead. He sat down beside her and pulled her to him, held her in his arms. She sighed gently.

"Abduallah. Well, he was so different to the other boys I'd known growing up."

"I'm sure. But not everyone seeks something different. Was what you knew so bad?"

She nodded and closed her eyes. "Imagine, Pittsburgh, winter, I was fourteen and wearing my mother's clothes out on a date." She half-laughed. "I had no idea how I looked but my boyfriend did. I pretended to laugh, to understand when he took me to the railway yards. It was only when he pushed me to the ground that I began to panic. It was cold, the ground was frozen and covered with the sharp stones. I thought he was playing at first." She shook her head in despair and the despair ground its way into his own body.

"God, I didn't even understand enough to know that when he forced me to have sex that he'd raped me. I believed him when he said I'd led him on; I believed him when he said that I shouldn't tell anyone because no one would accept the word of a cheap slut. But I didn't believe him when he said I had no future."

She shivered. "It was so cold," she continued. He followed her gaze up into the indigo desert sky where the stars shone with an intensity that made them swirl. "There were no stars in Pittsburgh that night. City lights obscured them I suppose. Or perhaps I just couldn't see them. I had to imagine them while I lay pinned down, looking up at the black sky."

He groaned and closed his eyes tight. He realized that she'd probably never told anyone her story before. He could tell by the way her words came out in a quiet stream as if she'd been holding back the flood of hurt for too long. If she'd found healing by telling him—and he hoped she had—then he'd found the opposite. Never had he felt such anger and pain and been unable to do anything about it. He felt the pain physically throughout his body. His hands hurt as he pulled her to him, holding her gently in arms that felt stiff with restraint.

"And then?"

"I stopped borrowing my mom's clothes that's for certain, avoided boys, avoided standing out at all and just studied hard. I learned how to blend into the background."

"The uniform of jeans and t-shirt; the uniform of Bedu robes," he suggested.

"Yeah."

"And you gained a scholarship to Cornell where you met Abduallah."

"Abduallah didn't try to put his hand up my skirt; he listened to me and I fell in love."

"You *did* love him then?"

"When he asked me to marry him I said yes. I had never imagined that I would find someone so caring. And then, after we married, I came to know him better, to understand him and I realized I loved him like a brother. He was my best friend." She stopped suddenly.

He frowned. "Like a brother? But—"

"Yes, Zahir?"

"But that was much later? Your love changed?"

He tried to find the answer in her eyes but she looked away as if not sure how to reply. He wanted her not to have been disloyal but the pieces didn't add up.

"Yes, my love changed. By the time I met you we were simply best friends."

He felt relieved but still a shadow of doubt dwelt in the back of his mind—a shadow he banished without further thought. There was no room in his life for doubt.

"I wanted you the moment I first saw you looking at me." His voice was rough with remembered lust.

"I thought I recognized you, thought I'd seen you somewhere else but perhaps it was the resemblance to Abduallah. Perhaps not…"

He turned her in his arms until she was looking up at him. The trust in her face melted his anger and dissipated the pain he felt at her story. He dipped his head, needing to physically connect with the woman to whom he was drawn like a parched man to water. It had been that way since their first meeting. But he couldn't kiss her immediately. He was close, so close that he could feel the warmth of her breath against his lips, so close that there was nothing between them except the communication between their eyes. He couldn't kiss her because he wanted to know that it was something she wanted. The imam didn't need to tell him to honor her because he already did.

She shifted her head to one side as if understanding the

unspoken question and nodded once, an imperceptible movement that registered loudly within him. But still he felt he couldn't move, couldn't break the spell of her. It was *her* lips that found his in a melding of warmth and softness and understanding. The kiss was like nothing before: not yet full of the passion that simmered beneath and not yet given over to the lust of their bodies, but holding more depth of feeling than he'd ever experienced.

It lasted about a minute. But he felt as if the sure ground upon which he'd built his life had shifted and nothing would be the same again. He pulled away and was relieved when she looked up at the stars. He followed her gaze noting distantly that the light of the stars spun out further in all directions than they had before, elongated by the mist that glazed his eyes.

He pulled her against him once more, his arm protectively around her, knowing that he could never let her go.

"I'm so sorry, Anna, for the past. I wish I'd known you then and could have protected you. No one should have gone through the pain of your childhood."

She smiled into his eyes. "Zahir. You can't protect everyone. You, yourself, had a childhood that was full of danger and hardship."

"It was my duty and my gift to my people."

"You were a boy, for God's sake."

He shook his head. "You will never understand."

"You're wrong. I do understand. I understand our differences—and our similarities—and that's Okay."

"Come, let's go to bed."

Anna lay in the large bed and waited. She could have gone to her own room. But she'd agreed to this marriage and she had never avoided the consequences of her decisions. So she lay there, listening to Zahir moving in the next room. Only the light of the stars illuminated the darkness. She watched his shadow slide into bed next to her. They lay in silence.

She reached out and touched his hand. It curled under hers and gripped hers with a need that she couldn't reciprocate now. She knew all it would take would be one indication from her, a caress, a movement, a word, a sign. But she couldn't do it. Why? She closed her eyes to see Abduallah's face, so clear in her mind. The day was finishing as it had begun with the person who stood between them.

Zahir didn't believe she understood much of their language, but she knew enough. And she also understood, probably at a deeper level than Zahir, the meaning of the imam's words. Honor had been in short supply when she'd been growing up. And in her future—whatever it might bring with Zahir—she was determined to not build her life on a lie. Zahir would know the truth about Abduallah, about Matta and herself, or else their marriage held no future.

She lay awake until late, much later than Zahir whose breathing soon quieted into the rhythm of sleep. She wanted him so much but she couldn't wish away all that had happened, no matter how much she might want to.

She looked out the window, catching glimpses of the wide sky with each snap and curl of the curtain. She wanted to see the stars. But clouds had started to roll across the desert sky and what had started off as a clear night had become overcast, leaving nothing but darkness.

CHAPTER 6

The week passed in a blur of smiling and dancing and eating and drinking with people Anna didn't know and doubted she would ever see again. But the family seemed pleased. Fatima was in her element, grinning from ear to ear and stepping in and taking charge of things when Anna either proved too inept or too disinterested.

It was the nights that Anna lived for. The quiet of the desert was beginning to grow on her. So different to New York where she'd shared a house with Abduallah after their divorce. New York, with its street noise—people, traffic, constant driven stress, was a world away from here. Here there was time to think, time to feel. And it was the nights that she saved for these moments. She lay beside Zahir night after night of that first week and still he didn't make a move toward her.

Slowly the haunting face of Abduallah appeared less often in her dreams as the healing power of tears and talk wrought their magic. But still she felt unable to bridge the physical and emotional gap between her and Zahir because the feeling of being trapped, unable to be free, to be fully herself —whatever that might be—remained strong.

By the end of the week Anna had become accustomed to sleeping with Zahir and awaking alone. But this morning was different. She lay for a few moments and wondered what was different, what the rhythmic patter was that she couldn't place. She looked at the clock. It was late—7am, much later than her usual 5am—and still dark. No brilliant sunlight invaded the room, no shrill, strange dawn calls of desert birds to remind her she wasn't in New York.

She looked around but a heavy silence reigned. Not even broken by a drifting of sound from elsewhere in the palace.

She rose and walked to the window. A heavy mist cloaked the palace and mountain, wreathing its mystery around the solid surfaces as if claiming them for its magic. Ragged tufts of mist drifted across the courtyard garden blown on a wind that was chill. Anna shivered and reached for Zahir's dressing gown.

Pulling the gown tight around her, she walked out into the courtyard. The paving was slippery and damp beneath her feet. The boughs hung heavy with water and brushed against her face as she walked under them. The water from the fountain seemed less important now, under the watery sky. She leaned back against the seat, relishing the chill of fresh water seeping onto her body from the low clouds, and let the damp caress her as if it were moist, cool towel on a hot day.

"Don't tell me you like this weather?"

She opened her eyes with a start. She hadn't heard Zahir enter the courtyard.

"I didn't in the States but here it's different." She closed her eyes briefly and inhaled the fragrant, moist air. "I didn't realize you had actual weather. I thought you only had sun."

He smiled. "Yes, we have weather. How else would my ancestors have survived without water?"

"You have the spring."

"Which was good for my father's ancestors whose palace this was. But my mother and her family were nomads, surviving on what little Allah granted them from these clouds."

"What can a brief shower do?"

He smiled. "I'll show you. It's about time you saw something of my country. Fatima has plans for Matta and his cousins for the next few days so we won't be missed."

It wasn't until the afternoon that they set off, just the two of them in his four-wheel drive. Her face was flushed with excitement as she scanned the horizon. For what, he did not know. He doubted even she knew. Her thirst for freedom was one thing he couldn't satisfy. Because to do so would mean letting her go and he wasn't prepared to do that. But he'd give her a taste of it.

"How far are we going?"

"Not far. It will take only a few hours."

"And you won't tell me where?"

"No. It's a surprise."

Her grin was as refreshing to his soul as the rain to the land, filling him with hope.

She dipped her head as flirtatiously as a bouncing car over rough terrain would allow. "I love surprises."

"Good."

Before long they turned off the main track onto a smaller rutted road that headed toward the mountains. He could feel the change of the air already against his skin and relaxed like he hadn't done in a very long time. He'd spent years camping out in these mountains, hiding, preparing for attack against the people who desired his land and all its riches. Places that had lain hidden to the outside world since biblical times, he and his people knew, and had kept hidden. It was their history, their land, their treasure.

They began winding their way up into the mountains along a wadi that now contained a swift-flowing river. At a point where the river opened up into a small valley Zahir stopped the car and they both jumped out. The usually arid valley was dusted with the fresh green of new growth.

He couldn't help but smile in response to Anna's incredulous expression as she looked around. It was as if the wadi had been touched by a magic wand. The small amount of rain that had fallen in the night had magically brought spring to the desert. The acacias and succulents were made a vivid green by the rain. The tracks of small mammals making the most of this sudden feast criss-crossed the surrounding sands and insects hovered and dipped around the bushes.

"It's amazing." She walked through the squat thorny caper bushes, her fingers gently brushing the fresh, green shoots while her eyes followed a dragonfly that flittered, iridescent, in the sunlight. "Is it always like this?"

"They've adapted over thousands of years to survive on morning dew. Usually the wadi is dry and there is no sign of life, but it's there, waiting for the rains to come. It takes little to bring life back to the desert. The recent rains are enough."

A lizard scuttled by. "Enough to sustain life for animals and people."

"It is why my people care for each other with their hospitality and sense of loyalty and duty. For much of the time there is nothing. And when there is this," he followed her gaze as she scanned the expanse of vibrant green that now clung to the usually dun-colored bushes. "We praise Allah for we are dependent on things outside of ourselves, things we cannot control."

"It's beautiful, like a miracle."

"Come back to the car, just a little further up into the mountains and we will be at our destination."

The four-wheel drive climbed higher, twisting and turning through seemingly impassable passes until they could go no further. As the sun lowered in the sky it shone its fiery red glow onto the yellow limestone making it look as if the light were emanating from the rock itself.

Zahir pulled up the vehicle beside a wall of rock.

"Hey, it's great. We've come all this way to look at," she waved her hand in a mock presentation, "a rock face".

"You like it?"

"Fabulous. It's a pale yellow, towering, rock. What more could I want?"

"I don't know. Let's see, shall we?"

He jumped out of the vehicle but before he could open her door she was already out and striding toward a narrow gap in the rock that was barely visible amongst the shadows.

"Hey! It's like a passage…"

He watched her as she passed through and stopped abruptly.

He came up behind her, his hands running down her arms, unable to stop himself from touching her now as they both stood looking at one of nature's miracles.

"Oh my God, it's wonderful." Anna's voice was soft with awe.

Zahir looked upon the complex of hot pools carved out of the stone above which steam rose. Around them were the ruins of old buildings that must have once seen crowds of people enjoying the thermal spa. Encircling the natural amphitheater, magnificent palm and tamarisk trees soared, beneath which the vegetation was lush, verdant, heavy with the moist atmosphere. To one side, above the old buildings, and beyond a small orange grove, a Bedu tent had been erected, its richly-woven canopies a decadent contrast to the pale yellow stone that alternated with red brick, still neat and intact.

"This is Ain Sukhna."

"How come I've never heard of this before?"

"Because we prefer to keep such treasures to ourselves."

"I'm not surprised."

He watched her walk around the edge of the site, as if too awed to move directly to the main bath that sat centrally, raised above the others. It would have been for the elite and the remains of columns lay at each point of a square around its edge that would originally have supported some form of pergola.

He leaned back against the rock face and watched her absorb its beauty. She brushed her hands through the luxuriant foliage of a tree and dabbled her fingers in the less warm water of a long, rectangular pool designed for swimming rather than for soaking.

Finally she sat on the edge of the central pool, surrounded by the warm steam and looked back at him, a broad smile across her face.

"Well you've certainly surprised me."

He came and stood before her.

"And you've surprised *me*."

She raised her eyebrows in query, shaking her head. "How?"

"Before, I wanted you. But now I know you, I want you more."

Her expression changed instantly, her eyes shone with emotion he could only describe as hope. It was as if his words had touched her somewhere deep, where the hurt of rejection for who she was, for where she came from, still lingered.

She reached over to him and he closed his eyes as he felt her tentative touch on his chest. Warm fingers slid up and spread over the scar over his heart, as if claiming it. Then the source of the heat that shot through his body, centering in his groin, was withdrawn.

"Look, up at the sky," she said softly.

He followed her gaze, dragging it away from what he really wanted to focus on, her. The early evening star was just beginning to emerge from its surrounding light, as if sucking in the last of the sun's rays.

"Venus," he said. "According to ancient Bedu legend the evening star is the male child of the moon and the sun."

He looked down at her and knew she was thinking of Matta. He drew her to him then, gently, despite his growing need for her. He knew it had to come from her.

"Come, let's bathe."

His hand dropped down her arm, relishing every inch of heated skin until he gripped her hand and pulled her over to the tent. "Everything we need is inside. I had it made ready for us earlier."

She laughed. "Of course you did. You know, Zahir, did anyone ever call you a control freak?"

"No they call me a sheikh."

"Perhaps it's the same thing."

"Perhaps."

He paused before the tent—its rich, woven geometric designs matched the ancient design of brick and stone that edged the pools and existing arches—and reluctantly let her hand drop. He pulled back the curtain of the tent and stood back for Anna to enter.

It was like an Aladdin's cave, Anna thought, straight out of a fairy tale. Richly-woven rugs with traditional designs covered the floor over which hung a brass, intricately decorated chandelier spiked with thick, white candles. There was nothing else—only a bed that occupied all the space. Anna dragged her eyes from the bed and explored the tent. Another flap revealed a wardrobe and yet another led to a mosaic lined, more modern bathroom. It was perfect.

"A bed. How convenient."

"I thought it might be useful—later."

"Umm. I am feeling a little tired."

"Not too tired to bathe, I hope?"

She grinned and desire lashed through her body when she saw his answering smile in his eyes that, for once, moved down to his mouth and flickered around his lips. She shook her head, unable to move her gaze from those lips.

"Then you should change." He tossed her a bikini she'd never seen before.

"That, is never for a grown woman." She pulled the tiny triangle of material as wide as it would stretch.

"For a grown woman, chosen by a grown man." He smiled again, a smile of unabashed sensuality. "I will leave you to get changed."

ANNA TWEAKED the tiny white triangles that covered her breasts down a little, trying to extend the material to cover all her breasts, but didn't succeed. She gave up, took a deep breath, and emerged into the soft light of dusk. Any embarrassment was immediately forgotten when she saw Zahir waiting for her, half naked. Although they'd been sharing a bed, he'd always come to bed and left again in the dark.

His rich skin seemed to shimmer under the reflection of torches that he'd lit around the main pool below them. She licked her lips but her mouth dried instantly at the sight of his muscled body and the two corded muscles down the sides of his hips that disappeared into his shorts.

When she dragged her eyes upwards to meet his own gaze she saw that his eyes were focused solely on her and they were hungry.

"You bought this bikini for me didn't you?"

He nodded. "I don't shop, Anna. But I did leave instructions for such an item to be bought. I thought it would suit you."

She felt his gaze down her body as if it were his nails dragging seductively down her skin until she felt her nipples harden in anticipation. She knew that they would easily be seen through the white flimsy material.

"And does it?"

He nodded once, his dark eyes fixed on her. He tore his eyes away and gestured for her to walk with him through the orange grove that led to the baths.

Heat from the ancient stone slabs that lined the path warmed Anna's bare feet. The thermal activity heated everything from the rocks, the soil, to the water. She ducked her head under a stray branch and emerged into a clearing lit by the torches, the bright stars above and a pale yellow sickle moon that hung low in the sky.

They walked up the wide steps into the hot pool and Zahir helped her down. The steps continued around the inner part of the pool, forming deep seats. The pool reflected the light of the stars and Anna sat back, the pool's heat and tangy mineral smell enveloping her.

"This," she breathed as she felt her muscles and mind relax, "is heaven."

When she opened her eyes, Zahir was lying alongside her, his body so close she could see the water lap and pool over his shoulders, his muscles gleaming under the light of the moon and the torches. His eyes were closed and she studied his face, so strong, like the rest of him, so beautiful when at rest. Gone was the strain of leadership and need. Only his innate strength was visible now.

He opened his eyes suddenly and her breath caught in her chest, tying knots in her throat. There was a vulnerability and a tenderness there that she'd seen only occasionally as the weeks had progressed. It had shown itself in slight hesitations where before there were none, in a flicker in the depth of the eye. But now the eyes that looked upon her were unveiled and calling into the depth of her soul. She took a deep, ragged breath and turned away. His gaze was too intimate. She felt it would annihilate her if she let it.

She looked fixedly up at the stars, aware that he was now looking at her with the same intensity.

She wanted him now. She didn't want to build their life together on lies. She wanted the truth, she wanted to honor him as the imam said.

"I've never seen such stars." She turned to him once more. "You know, as a girl I was obsessed with stars, I used to know them all, the constellations, the planets, the far-away stars, but I could only ever see a few."

"Why would you be so interested in what you couldn't see?"

"Because I knew that beyond the darkness were beautiful things, better and brighter than I knew. I needed to know that they were there. At university and later, in New York City, I still used to search for them but it was too bright in the city."

"So are they as beautiful as you imagined?"

She didn't speak for a long time because her mind was a whirl of images and feelings that spun together, resolving themselves into a different shape: her love for her son, her need for freedom. Only weeks ago she'd been afraid she was losing both. Now she knew she'd never lose her son and she had a nagging feeling that perhaps she'd found more freedom here, with Zahir, than she ever had before. Perhaps not enough—but still more.

"More so."

"You look thoughtful. What are you thinking of?"

She smiled, not willing to open her thoughts so completely yet to him. "That I found it hard to leave Matta tonight."

"He reminds you of Abduallah, doesn't he?"

She looked up into his eyes unable to believe that he truly could not see that Matta was his child.

"No. That wasn't it. He really doesn't look much like Abduallah."

"He has his coloring."

She briefly raised her eyebrows and sighed.

"Zahir, I—"

But he silenced her with a finger that brushed her lips and took away her thoughts. She closed her eyes, her mouth parting under the gentle pressure of his finger that circled her lips before the tip of his finger rubbed back and forward along her lower lip. The tip of her tongue found his finger, before her lips closed around it, sucking lightly before kissing it. She could feel the heat building in her, was aware of the sharp intake of his breath as she sucked his finger.

All her thoughts and intentions slipped away as his hot breath quickened against her skin. They moved together, their lips finding each other's in a kiss that had none of the gentleness of their previous kiss, none of the delicacy and none of the hesitancy. Like the welling up of the thermal water from deep within the hot earth, their passion came from somewhere deep inside where it had been building its heat, heightening its pressure until it was ready to explode.

As their mouths searched each other's for the connection from which they'd both held back for so long, Zahir pulled her through the water into his arms. Straddled across his lap, his arms around her, the barrier between them broken at last, Anna wanted nothing more than for the final barrier between them to be gone. Her lips opened wide to allow his tongue entry to caress hers; her arms pulled him tighter to her so she could feel his hard, muscled chest pressing against her soft breasts and the strength of his arousal pressing against her body.

But no amount of closeness seemed to be enough. They were both feverish with desire. His hands pushed up inside her bikini top, exposing her breasts to his lips, his mouth, his tongue. Lightning flashes fired through her as his impatient hands slid under her bikini bottom and tore them off, the loose knots easily giving way to his impatient hands.

Naked, on top of him, Anna could feel his need for her clearly through his shorts. It was her turn to yank them off and as they floated down the pool to join her bikini, she eased herself forward until he was touching her: his breath upon hers, her breasts upon his chest and her sex upon his, touching him, driving them both crazy with need.

The warm water surged around them as Zahir reached behind him and plucked a condom from a robe pocket. With shaking hands she tore the wrapper; with impatient hands he slid it into place and slipped back into the pool again. She raised herself into the cooler air, her skin and nipples peaking, before she plunged down on top of him.

She trembled at the sensation of his flesh inside hers. Her skin felt tight with need. Her hands, her feet, her shoulders, her breasts, tingled with nerve endings made electric by the smooth slide of him against her most sensitive skin.

She could feel the pulse of him from deep within him, surfacing deep within her. She hardly dared to move for fear of the devastating sensations that made her lose herself, made her feel that she was disintegrating.

But she wasn't disintegrating; she was complete. One look into his eyes in which she could see herself reflected back as if she filled him as much as he was filling her, told her that. As they moved together, she could feel the beat of his heart beneath her hands, echoing her own rapid heartbeat.

But with each shift of her body up and down onto his, she felt her body lose that grounding connection with the physical as it turned as liquid as the water that pumped around them. It was only his strong arms holding her that kept her upright—and the fact that she could no more stop creating the sensations that devastated her body and mind, than stop breathing. He sat up and held her then and she fell back into arms that were strong and yet gave her the room to surrender to the feeling of total bliss that exploded inside and swept out and engulfed her whole being. Her cries, immediately followed by his, carried around the clearing, bouncing off the walls that enclosed them, before drifting up with the steam, up into the stars.

She stopped moving and fell against him, still connected, still aware of every movement of his hard body inside her, on the edge of her. He lifted her chin and kissed her tenderly on the lips before he withdrew, picked her up in his arms and stepped out of the bath. Water fell from them both in heavy rivulets, withdrawing its heat from her overheated body and allowing the cooler air to spike her body with new sensations: sensations that the movement of Zahir's hands only increased.

Within minutes Zahir had set her down on a soft rug beside the pool, strewn with cushions. He kissed her once more but her hand sought out what she wanted and he groaned as she caressed him before pulling him closer to where she wanted him. He frowned briefly before ripping open another packet and this time her fingers didn't hesitate as she pulled it down onto him with both hands caressing him. She dropped onto her back and he plunged deep within her as her legs came around to capture his body, pressing him into her. But any sense of capture was fleeting. He controlled her: physically, pushing her body rhythmically against the cushions, and emotionally, holding her gaze with eyes that held only a reflection of her own star-lit eyes, until the twisting spirals of sensation flared and shot through her body as she called out his name. Only then did he climax, pulsing into her with a cry that shot straight into her heart.

She kept her legs wrapped around him tight, not wanting the intimacy to end, not wanting him to withdraw but he did. And he kissed her then with an all-encompassing tenderness that made her realize that the intimacy hadn't ended, it had only just begun.

SHE AWOKE INSIDE THE TENT. She scarcely remembered returning there. But she remembered the love-making that had followed throughout the night. Thinking back to the weeks she'd spent at the palace, she couldn't believe she'd waited so long for him. Yet she knew that she'd needed that time to come to terms with her own emotions.

As the soft gray light morning stole into the tent, she looked across at Zahir. He was sleeping peacefully but as soon as she sat up, his eyes flicked open. She laughed.

"Don't you ever sleep deeply?"

He shook his head. "Years of living in the desert; years of having to be alert to danger—I cannot rid myself of the habit."

"It's a useful habit because it makes things quite easy for me. Just one movement and I have you where I want you." Her hand slid under the sheet and stroked him. He closed his eyes and groaned.

"Haven't you had enough for one night, woman?"

"No. And nor have you apparently." She marveled at his rigid thickness that she held in her hand. It echoed the shape of his body: thick and strong and full of a simmering passion that needed only her touch to kick into life.

Her naked breasts tightened with the chill of the morning air—and desire—and she wriggled closer to him until the heat that rolled off his body completely enveloped her and she sighed. She moved her hand up his body, over his hard-toned muscles and chest until her hand lay briefly over his heart. She wriggled closer again until her head lay against his chest and she could both feel and hear the quickened thud of his heart pushing the blood to where he needed it most.

She reached over to the box of condoms and smoothly rolled one onto him before sliding one leg around him. Lying on top of him, her body tight against his, her head against his chest, she was filled with a sense of utter bliss—of warmth and comfort and simple rightness—that shocked her. Quickly she slid down onto him and stopped, watching his face. He watched her through narrowed eyes, the only movement coming from inside her, heightening the sensations that spread deliciously through her body. As she moved slowly, teasingly on him, his face tightened with pleasure. She continued to move on him determined to see him climax, as he always did her. But her control was no match for his and the wave after wave of shimmering release hit her before he allowed himself the same release.

She rolled over into his arms, their heads close. She'd never felt so close to anyone in her whole life. And this man was her husband.

She trailed her fingertips along his body and watched the hair follicles rise in response to the light scrape of her nails. She moved and bent down and skimmed her lips along the same trail, kissing the skin, warming it with her breath. The tent was cool in the morning and her breath clouded slightly.

"Anna. I need to tell you something. The first condom, I'm not sure if it protected you. The pressure of the water around us may have made it ineffective."

Shocked, Anna didn't speak.

"We risked much last time," Zahir continued, "thank God nothing came of it."

She suddenly felt angry. How dare he say that? Matta had come of it and she couldn't even begin to imagine not wanting Matta.

"And *I* need to tell you something. I know I should be worried about the risk involved but I can't be. Because a large part of me—not the practical part that's for sure—doesn't want anything to come between us. No barriers, no lies."

She paused, searching his face for a reaction, but finding only a blank mask that chilled her. "Go on." His voice, too, was distant now.

"Matta…"

"What about Matta? He's well isn't he?"

She nodded, drawing up all her courage and resolve to continue. "Of course. I need to tell you that Matta is your son. He was six weeks premature—a difficult pregnancy…"

He continued to look at her but she could see the shock register in his eyes as her words stopped, waiting for his response.

"You *need* to tell me?" His voice was soft, holding within it a violence that frightened her. He turned from her then and shifted away from her awkwardly as he sat up, looking away from her.

"I tried to tell you."

"Obviously not hard enough."

She reached out to him. "Please, don't do this. Not after

what we've just experienced together. We have a new beginning, a new chance."

He swung around to face her then. "Based on lies? Anna, have you not understood anything about me and about the code by which I live my life? Lying has no part in it. I have always wanted the truth from you. And you have never given it." He raked his fingers through his hair, moving away from her again. But she could see the vibration of the low groan filter down his back. "You tell me my nephew is, in fact, my son—a fact you have kept from me for six years—and think I should forget this small oversight of yours and continue as before?" He shook his head and stared at her. She flinched beneath his icy gaze. "It doesn't work like that."

She fell back into bed under the blow of his gaze. She shook her head. "I thought—"

"What exactly *did* you think?"

"You said that nothing could come between us. You said you wanted to know the truth. I have told you the truth."

"All of it?"

She couldn't answer. Because telling the truth about Abduallah would betray his memory and destroy the image of Abduallah that had given Zahir his motivation and rationale all during the war years, and that still lingered now, like a silent sentinel to his heart. One word from her and the sentinel would disappear, destroying the strong, sure lines that delineated Zahir's world.

"I thought so. When will the lies cease?"

Long silent moments drew longer but neither moved nor spoke before he rose, turning to her only once. "I will have a car come for you within the hour."

A cool blast of air enveloped her as he drew open the door to the tent and went outside without a further word.

CHAPTER 7

Zahir watched Anna leave, her stiff figure unmoving in the back seat of the four-wheel drive. She didn't turn around.

He looked away deliberately. He chose not to see anymore but he couldn't choose not to hear the sound of the retreating vehicle as it revved and roared over the stony ground, down through the twists and turns of the wadi before emerging onto the plains. Taking his lying wife with it.

Six years. For six years she'd kept the fact that he was a father secret from him. How could he ever forgive her?

He'd thought he could overlook her disloyalty to his brother, somehow come to terms with her character that was so opposite to his own. But now this, on top of Abduallah's death.

How could he ever trust her again?

He looked out beyond the vehicle to the smudge of mountains that indicated where the palace was. There was nothing between the two sets of mountains except desert. He breathed deeply of the dry heat that swept off the plains, striving to neutralize the bitterness and anger that he could feel filling his veins.

This was his life: guardian of his people and his family and his land. He'd never wanted a child. How could a cold man care properly for one? If ever he had any softer feelings, they had been knocked out of him by the loss of his mother and the fighting he'd thrown himself into for years. They'd made him the man he'd become; a man fit to be an uncle maybe, but not fit to be a father. And he wasn't fit to be a husband either. But he was both now and his control of the situation was slipping away as surely as the sand through his fingers.

Confusion, anger, frustration at his inability to control the situation engulfed him. But he'd never run, or hidden from anything. He'd face things but not yet, not while he couldn't control his feelings.

ANNA CLOSED her dry eyes against the stinging dust. She couldn't have cried even if she'd wanted to. The shock of his emotional retreat left her numb. How could she have been such a fool to believe he'd understand?

When the car stopped she opened her eyes slowly and gazed up at the palace walls that soared high all around them, a soft yellow against a brilliant cerulean sky. It was the same place she'd come to weeks ago and yet it wasn't. Now, it was home.

She didn't see the building in isolation anymore, but in relation to the plains, to the hidden oases, and communities of the desert. It was a part of Zahir's world, not enclosed within itself.

She half-laughed to herself—another strategy no doubt, to make her feel she wasn't trapped. But she felt more trapped than ever and it had nothing to do with any buildings or countries, any physical boundaries. She was obsessed with someone who didn't care for her and never would.

It was gone midnight by the time Zahir returned. But instead of going directly to his own room he went to Anna's. He knew she'd be there—either not expecting his return or not wanting, or being able to, face him again. But she would have to face him because he wanted answers.

Starlight lit Anna's bright hair. Darkness and shadows pooled all around but her hair seemed to glow dull silver under the incandescent light of the stars. She looked like a fallen angel lying there, disheveled as if dreaming disturbing dreams, the sheet twisted around her shifting legs, her arms reaching out for something that was beyond her.

He felt the now familiar grip in his chest as if whatever it was that she was reaching for she'd found—within him. He stepped back, shocked by the depth of his need. The sound of his feet on the floor must have awoken her because she suddenly sat upright, still dazed by sleep.

"Zahir?"

"How can you be sure he isn't Abduallah's child?"

She pushed herself up in bed, pushed her hair out of her eyes and sighed. "Believe me, I know. I am one hundred percent positive that you are Matta's father."

He felt his shoulders relax with relief. When she'd first told him he'd been angry because he was scared he wouldn't be enough for Matta. But the anger had swiftly disappeared, followed by a fear that there may have been a mistake—that Matta wasn't his—and he could no more bear that than live in exile from his home.

"Did Abduallah believe Matta to be his?"

"No."

Zahir felt a further surge of relief tainted with guilt.

"He knew Matta to be mine?"

"I don't know. I think so, yes."

"You need to tell me everything."

Anna swung her legs off the bed and walked around the room, avoiding getting too close to him. "OK. Abduallah, he —" she looked at him once and then sighed heavily, as if unsure, "he knew it couldn't have been him. There was no possibility. He never asked me who the father was and I never told him but I think he knew. And I also think he believed, from your attitude to me, that you had no further interest in me."

"And so you didn't consider I'd be interested to know I'd fathered a son." His voice was quiet.

"It wasn't that."

"What was it?"

"I didn't *want* you to know."

Zahir's turned away from her, stiff with anger. "And so because on a whim—"

"No whim. I knew you'd take him away from me, away from us—"

"Of course I would."

"Then you can hardly blame me for not telling you."

"I blame you. I blame you for making sure I believed you were two months pregnant with Matta when we met that night in Paris. You told that lie to Abduallah knowing he'd tell me. You led me to believe Matta was a full-term baby and that Abduallah was his father."

"I'm sorry. I don't expect you to understand but from the moment I felt Matta move in my stomach I knew that I would do anything for that child, but most of all I would love him and keep him close. I couldn't let you take him."

"I did anyway."

They fell into a deep silence, one that nothing could fill. He felt Anna's tentative touch on his shoulder.

"Zahir." Her voice was soft and he closed his eyes, wanting to reach out to her but knowing that nothing could be said or felt or done to take away the lies of the past.

He stepped back, his hand in the air, making a barrier between them. "No. I have to go."

"It's up to you now. You have to either come to terms with this—or not."

Or not. Her words stayed in his mind as he closed the door behind him and returned to his empty room.

∽

"No!" Matta said irritably, frowning at his mother who wasn't concentrating as well as he expected her to.

"I'm sorry, honey. Right, show me again."

Anna was trying to concentrate on the song and actions that Matta was showing her, but failing spectacularly. Three days had passed since she'd seen Zahir. No sign. Not a word.

She was living in some surreal state of limbo from which she couldn't seem to surface to function normally.

"Hmm," Matta said, his mouth twisting and his brow lowering in a characteristic movement she recognized from Zahir. "Mom, that's no good." He smiled with sympathy at her. "Perhaps you'd better leave it to me."

Anna laughed at his adult words. He was like a sponge, absorbing something from everyone around him: the language from the adults and the fun from his cousins and friends. She ruffled his hair and he shrugged from her reach.

"Perhaps I better had." At least the three days had allowed her to give her undivided attention to Matta, admiring the new talents he was learning, taking extra pleasure from his love, a love that hadn't seemed to diminish, despite her fears, but seemed to grow. She needed that now, more than ever. "Come here and give me a hug."

A resigned Matta shuffled forward and bent his head to be kissed and hugged. He patted her on the back in a gesture she knew to be one of dismissal. She couldn't help but laugh. She hugged him tight and, teasingly, wouldn't let him go.

"Mom, I have to go now. Ab Zahir is going to take me out with the falcons."

Her heart thudded at the mention of Zahir and she let Matta slip from her arms.

"I don't like you playing with the falcons."

"Mom, it's not playing. It's part of our culture, that's what Ab Zahir says. Besides he will be there."

Quite, Anna thought. For the first time since their return she knew where he would be.

"And so will I."

ANNA PAUSED FOR A FEW MOMENTS, struck by the image of loneliness that Zahir made, as he stood with his back to them, his white robes, rippling in the breeze, outlined vividly against the blue sky and the wide empty expanse.

He turned suddenly at the sound of Matta's running feet and lifted him into the air before pulling him into a bear hug that brought a lump to Anna's throat. She knew that Matta had been spending time with Zahir but hadn't witnessed firsthand their increasing closeness.

On some level, Zahir was coming to terms with being a father. And Matta certainly saw Zahir as his second father. From what Matta called him—Ab, or Father, Zahir—she knew that he saw him as such.

"Zahir?"

She tried to keep her face and voice from trembling and assumed she must have succeeded as Zahir looked not in the least disturbed.

"Anna." He nodded in distant greeting.

"I would like to come along, if I may."

"As you like."

Anna could feel a knot like a sob inching its way up her chest at the icy chill of his tone.

Matta looked from one to the other and his brows were knitted but he made no comment.

Anna fell into step with Matta between them, listening to Matta's chatter and Zahir's indulgent comments. As they reached the falconry, Matta ran forward and turned, his face turning from excitement to concern at the sight of both of them, close yet miles apart.

"Mom, what's the matter with Ab Zahir and you? Did you get cross with him because he did something wrong?"

"What do you mean?"

"It's just that Ab Zahir looks how I feel when I've done something wrong and you tell me off. You shouldn't tell him off. He's the sheikh."

Anna felt her jaw drop with the injustice of his accusation but she was unable to form any words except look at Zahir whose eyes were full of laughter.

When she turned back to Matta, he had disappeared into the depth of the falconry leaving them alone.

"What is your western expression? Out of the mouths of babes?"

"Comes absolute, uninformed rubbish! I *should* tell you off because you're behaving badly. Yes, I probably should have told you that Matta was your child but you know what? If I had my time again I'd do exactly the same thing. He was my child, his birth father wanted nothing to do with me and his adopted father wasn't well and I—"

"Yes, I know—"

"I had to do…" she paused mid-sentence, dumb-founded. "You know? What are you saying?"

"Matta has talked about your life together in New York. I

know a little of what you went through. He's talked about Abduallah and he's talked about you. He's a bright boy."

"Of course he is. He has my genes."

He smiled at her. "And mine."

"And that must be what makes him such a rascal."

"No it's what makes him unable to trust unless that trust is earned."

"He trusts me."

His eyes flickered around her face, as if searching for something.

"And I want to, too."

"Then try to understand."

Anna turned and walked away abruptly before the tears she could feel welling behind her eyes began to fall. The walk quickened as soon as she was out of his sight and she ran blindly back into the palace, not stopping until she reached her office. She ran in and slammed the door closed on the world behind her, leaned back against the door and sobbed for the man she wanted but who would make no effort to understand her.

SHE LAY in bed that night, her hot eyes closed, the cool breeze upon her heated skin, her mind full of the light of the stars and the white flowers that lit the desert after rain. She only seemed to see the light when her eyes were closed. One day she hoped she'd open them and see such beauty. But for now, she dare not think of anything else but held on to that image while the emotions ebbed and flowed within.

It had been like this since she'd left him at the oasis. The hours passed in this ageless place moving like the sand, always shifting and changing, but always looking the same. She'd never been more acutely aware of the sensation of waiting. Waiting for understanding to come to him—or desire. Waiting for a miracle. But none came.

Was it all over so quickly? Had his passion been so slight that one night together had been sufficient to extinguish it?

Some time after midnight she fell into a restless doze, her dreams full of the light of desert blooms, her heart full of hope. Suddenly she awoke, her senses alert. She lay quite still, dazed, wondering for a moment where she was, wondering what had awoken her. There was no sound, no shape in the dark room. But she knew it was him. Silently he slipped onto the bed beside her.

"Anna." She closed her eyes briefly, melting at his voice, and his touch as he sat on the bed beside her, his hands reaching out for her, pulling her to him. All her anger and hurt at his coldness was forgotten by the reality of his presence.

He pushed his hands through her hair and cradled her face for one long moment, before he brought his lips to hers, holding her still so he could take all that he wanted. She felt as if she'd been lost in the desert until that moment, dying inch by inch under the sweltering, lifeless sun.

She couldn't do anything other than give him as much as he wanted—and more. As their mouths and tongues continued to search for satisfaction, in a restless, anguished passion of twisting, turning, pressure of lips against lips, of body against sliding body, she felt his heart beat against hers. She felt powerful, raised by electricity, shimmering with awareness, shot through with need.

He rose suddenly and walked away from the bed. Anna could barely hear the tear of a packet above the panting of her breath. He was back with her in seconds and she wrapped her legs around him, hooking him and bringing him close to her. He pulled away from her kiss. And for one long moment they looked at each other in the shallow darkness where emotions were more tangible than the vague outline of the physical. But she could see his eyes, black and white, intense and demanding. His eyes didn't just hold promise but delivered it. They made love to her as surely as his body was about to. She felt the connection, intimate, strong, and erotic as surely as if he'd penetrated her. She gasped and her legs trembled around him.

His gaze didn't shift from hers as his hands smoothed down her trembling legs, lending them strength as he shifted and lifted them both around her and entered her. She climaxed with his first thrust, which he held there, deep inside her, as she opened her mouth to cry out but his mouth robbed her of sound, muting her ecstasy as her whole body trembled around his. Only when the trembling ceased did he move: rhythmic, unrelenting, moving in and out of her, each movement as intense as the last. It was a claiming. And she wanted to be claimed.

Still he watched her but now she had a sense of his own passion over-riding his need to enjoy her need. She could see it in his eyes, concentrated, his focus shifting from hers into a place of unknown feeling, shifting inside himself as he surrendered to his passion; as he passed his control over to his body and to her body, united in their passion.

She climaxed again, with loud moans of pleasure and Zahir's finger tracing her lips as they cried out. Only then did Zahir release his own pleasure, quietly, as if a reflection of the inner nature of his climax. As his eyes re-focused on her she could see that a wall had fallen away. There was a different quality to his expression. Open, connecting with her on a different level.

He rolled away and as they lay quietly side by side, their bodies slick with sweat, the rapid beat of their hearts beginning to subside, her hand reached for his body, feeling the scar that lay above his heart.

"I'm sorry." His words came to her so quietly that she felt they must have been her own.

She shifted onto her side, looking at him as he gazed up at the ceiling.

"I'm sorry," he repeated. "For everything. For losing control that night six years ago; for being so bitter when I discovered who you were; for being so angry with you. I'm also sorry that you couldn't tell me about Matta but I understand."

The simplicity of his apology shocked her. But, more than that, she desperately wanted to know how Zahir now felt about Matta, whether her deception had changed his affection for him. But she dared not ask.

"I've hated not being able to tell you. It's a relief for you to know. I feel I've been carrying around this huge secret for so long."

"Tell me, how did Abduallah feel about looking after someone else's baby?"

"He loved him. Our, *situation*, was complicated but he understood. And he loved him. He'd never thought he would have a child so Matta seemed like a gift from heaven."

"Me also. I have wanted a child all my life but felt I could never be a proper father to children, a proper husband to a wife."

"How could you think that?"

He looked at her then with a thousand years of tiredness in his eyes. "Because," his hand clasped hers that still lay over his scar, "if I have a heart at all, it is cold; it is dead."

She shook her head in vehement denial. "No. That's not true."

"Anna," he stroked her hair with a look of tenderness lightening the weariness in his eyes. "It *is* true. I have killed and been nearly killed. I have taken those lessons to the financial markets and been ruthless in my pursuit of my country's wealth. These are not the things I would wish a child of mine to do."

"You said yourself that you did what you had to do."

He nodded. "And I believed it was my fate not to have children. But now, you have given me a gift more precious than you could know or I could have imagined."

"And Matta? Tell me, how do you feel about him now?"

"I have no change in my feelings toward him."

Anna's heart dropped.

"I couldn't feel more for him than I do already."

Anna couldn't speak. He didn't use the word "love" but she didn't care because in his own way he was telling her that he did love Matta. And that meant the world to her. Because she'd been terrified that he would resent this innocent child whose paternity had been kept secret from him.

They lay in silence for a long moment—a silence broken only by the sounds of a night owl laying claim to its prey; the soft murmur of the water in the courtyard and the rustle of leaves in the bushes outside their window. She felt his hand reach out for hers and caress hers before holding it tightly as if he never wanted to let go.

"Kiss me Anna." His voice was hoarse with emotion. "Say you forgive me."

Her mouth found his in the darkness and accepted his apology in an expression that was far more eloquent than words.

~

THEIR DAYS SLIPPED into a pattern of passionate love-making at night and also, now, during the day wherever they happened to meet or wherever they arranged to meet—the cave of the spring, lonely, forgotten corners of the ancient palace, or a bed of soft, blooming flowers. Wherever was handy and private that they could vent the lust that their night-time love-making seemed only to arouse further.

It was all as he had predicted. He was getting what he'd wanted all along—her in his bed. And he was riding out his obsession for her all right. Just the thought of him, only hours before, impatient hands pushing up her dress, free of the underwear she'd taken to not wearing, and lifting her up so he could enter her, his hands gripping her bottom as he thrust into her, pushing into the very soul of her, pinning her against the wall of a forgotten part of the palace—dust-filled, lofty, and majestic—unable to wait for the night ahead.

She groaned with renewed arousal and tried to concentrate on her books that were strewn across the desk before her. Despite the passionate sex, there was the dull clanging of an alarm bell ringing in her mind. He was always so busy, so preoccupied with state business that they barely talked. Their relationship was almost wholly physical. He was riding out his passion for her, just as he'd imagined. But if or when he was sated, what then? Anna had the suspicion that Zahir kept it purposely at this physical level, unwilling to accept her on a more emotional level. Why, she didn't know. But she found it hard to ignore a nagging sense of inferiority. She didn't come from his world, in any sense. So what would happen if he grew bored? Would it all end, just as he'd predicted? Would he move on to another wife and what would she have left if he did?

She flipped through the pages of a textbook irritably. She'd have nothing, only whatever she could create for herself from the wreckage of their passion. And at the moment she was concentrating on Matta—her pride and joy —and her studies.

Matta was continuing to blossom under the care and guidance of his extended family. But he still came to her first for love. Her fears of him moving away from her were unfounded, she now realized. He had a big heart with plenty of room for everyone in it, but with a special place that would always be hers.

She smiled at the gap-toothed photo of Matta she kept on her desk, nudging it closer with her pen. He was going to become the image of Zahir, with his build and coloring. But his nature was different. He had the ability to charm people with a happy-go-lucky quality that Zahir certainly didn't possess and that she had faint memories of growing up. Given a different upbringing perhaps she also would have had this talent for happiness.

And her studies were going well. She received daily deliveries from Riyadh of textbooks, notes, monographs, and research. It was, after all, the key to her freedom and her future when Zahir grew tired of her. Despite the emotional upheaval, or because of it, her studies proved the one constant that kept her going. She was looking forward to the Paris trip she'd arranged to attend a week of intensive tutorials at the Sorbonne's law school.

She dropped her pencil and gazed out to the garden, now sweltering under the summer sun. Matta would enjoy Paris. As well as her studies, she'd arranged time for just the two of them to hang out together. His nurse would come of course, for when she attended the university but, without Zahir, there would be no need for the usual entourage of security. She hadn't had a chance to mention it to Zahir but assumed he wouldn't care one way or the other. When he wasn't making love to her he was totally consumed with politics and business. He had no time in his life for anything else.

Suddenly the door to her study was flung open and Zahir strode in, a look of thunder on his face.

"What is this about you taking Matta to Paris without my permission?"

"I need your permission now? You knew I was going. You didn't think I was going to leave Matta behind, did you?"

"You should have told me of your intentions."

"I didn't think it worth bothering you with. You've been so preoccupied. Besides when should I have told you? We don't do anything that involves conversation at night or day. When, exactly, do you think I should have raised this?"

"You could have written to me."

She exploded. "Written you a note. Of course. That's how all husbands and wives communicate. By writing notes. Zahir! You are impossible. Why will you never speak to me? Why do you still keep your distance from me when we can't keep our hands off each other when we are alone? No, don't answer that. I know why."

"Why?"

She raised her eyebrows and shrugged, perfecting that nonchalant attitude when she was dying inside. "Because you want me for sex and you hate yourself for wanting someone like me."

"You're wrong."

She looked up expectantly, daring not to hope. "No, I don't suppose you do hate yourself."

"How can you think so little of yourself to imagine I would not be proud to want you for yourself—all of you, your past and present." He gripped her shoulders. "Do you hear me, Anna? All of you. It is *you* who hate yourself."

"Then why the distance?"

He let go and shrugged lightly. "That is my character and you will have to accustom yourself to that. I am who I am, as you are who you are. I accept you, now you must accept me."

"I don't have much chance when I see you only for stolen moments during the day and at night when we have other things on our mind."

"Then that will change, will it not, when I come to Paris with you."

"No. I'm going alone with Matta and Muma Yemena. Just us."

"And why would you want that?"

"Just for some quiet, normal time with my son."

"*Our* son." He opened the door behind him. "And I *am* coming."

"To control me, to control Matta? That's it isn't it?"

She waited for an answer that didn't come.

"Just accept it, Anna. I *am* coming."

He closed the door leaving her alone and in emotional turmoil once again. She was obviously correct. His need to control surpassed everything.

Zahir walked with his usual sense of purpose through the reception rooms back toward his office, knowing there was nothing about him that reflected the turmoil he kept locked inside. And that was how he liked it.

She was wrong. He kept his distance from her because he had no choice. He couldn't risk coming closer to her, easing the sadness that he still felt lay deep inside of her. Because the one thing that would ease her pain was the one thing he could never admit. He rubbed his hand on his scar, feeling the heartbeat underneath. Scar tissue strengthened the skin, effectively sealing whatever was underneath by an ugly, but well nigh impenetrable, barrier. He had no idea what lay beneath the scar and he had no intention of ever finding out.

And she was also wrong about his wish to accompany her to Paris. It wasn't his need to control that made him want to go with her. It was fear. Fear that she would leave him.

CHAPTER 8

Zahir couldn't take his eyes off Anna.
She sat opposite him, looking out the window at the gray clouds as they descended into Charles de Gaulle Airport. Her eyes were bright, lit from inside, in a way that made him sad. He hadn't seen her like that in Qawaran, despite the fact that she had seemed to blossom there. His eyes flicked to her breasts, where the nap of her silk shirt gleamed where it pulled slightly when she moved. He felt himself stir, wanting her just as he always wanted her. He thought once they were lovers then his need for her would lessen. But, he thought, grimly, it was intensifying if anything and getting more out of control. He hated being out of control. He scowled and followed her gaze.

"You don't like Paris?" Anna obviously mistaking the cause of his scowl.

"It's a city, like any other."

She smiled and gazed back at the city that was coming into view beneath them.

"Well, if you don't like it, then why come? Think I'll run off with your son?"

"What would be the point? There is nowhere you can hide from me. I would find you as I found you before. And you know that."

He watched her swallow and a moment of panic flit across her face. He sat back and sighed. He was annoyed with himself. It was a low blow. He was angry with her because he wanted her so much and his need was growing in ways he couldn't control, ways he didn't wish to consider. But he still didn't need to have taunted her with her lack of freedom.

She soon recovered though and met his gaze with an equally irritated one.

"Then why are you here? You always seem to have too much to do in Qawaran. I'm surprised you could get away. Don't tell me that it's my allure that's pulled you away from all things important."

"I have business in Paris." Her face fell slightly and he felt its echo more loudly within himself.

"I see."

The tilt of her chin as she looked out at the patchwork of fields below touched him.

He leaned forward, cupped her chin with his fingers and drew her face round to his, searching the large expressive, blue-gray eyes that failed to hide her feelings.

"But nothing I couldn't have accomplished from Qawaran. I wanted to be with you."

His blood raced as her eyes, full of hope, traced his lips. "I'm glad you came."

Her eyes were dark with anticipated passion.

He sank back into his chair and closed his eyes, trying to control his need to take her then and there.

"Talk to me, Anna. About anything."

She laughed, able to read his mind. "Paris then. It's like coffee and cream."

He shook his head. "You, Anna, are obsessed with food

these days. You must be, because I've heard Paris described in many ways but none like that."

"No really. It's such a creamy city. I remember the first time I came here with Abduallah." Her quick glance at him was to check to see if he resented the reference to Abduallah. Despite his love for his brother he couldn't help feeling a twist of jealousy. He controlled it instantly. "I thought it more beautiful than anything I'd ever seen. The light was so soft, the buildings so old and grand, the people so chic."

He closed his eyes so he could see better what she was describing. "It's all that—and more."

"And I met you here."

He felt himself draw away. "What I never understood was why Abduallah wasn't keeping you company that evening in the hotel bar. Where was he?"

She blinked softly, looking down at the flat plain beyond which the city glinted through a misty haze. But he knew she wasn't thinking about the city, her gaze was too abstracted.

"Zahir. Don't you understand? He was with friends. We weren't together then. We weren't a couple but he wanted to pretend we were, for your sake."

"For my sake. What are you talking about?"

"Abduallah, he—"

"Didn't want to admit that his marriage had failed?"

She raised her eyebrows briefly. "Something like that."

He didn't understand her resigned tone. "He shouldn't have worried. These things happen. And it would have made things easier between you and me."

"I couldn't betray him."

He flicked a strand of hair back over her shoulder. "And there was me thinking you *had* betrayed him."

"No. I had only betrayed myself."

"And what is that meant to mean?"

"It was the first time, since that time I spoke to you about, when I was fourteen, that I had been with a man."

"Apart from Abduallah, you mean?"

She sighed. "Let's change the subject." She took his hand as they both looked out the window. "Paris. It's a city for walking." She looked around at the door beyond which she knew the bodyguards were relaxing. "Do they have to go everywhere with us?"

"Of course."

"But wouldn't it be nice, just for once, if we were alone? I want you. All to myself."

He laughed. "You are a greedy, selfish girl."

She loved it when he laughed. She studied his face. The lines were relaxed and humor sparkled in his eyes. His short hair had grown longer recently and fell back from his face in soft waves until it just skimmed his collar. She pushed her fingers through it, not only enjoying the feel of the thick hair through her fingers, but enjoying the flare of sensuality that ignited in his eyes at her touch. She sat back opposite him purposefully.

"Greedy am I? Perhaps I should stop being so greedy. Yes, I wouldn't want you to think me so out of control."

"Woman," he growled, "this is the only time I'm telling you not to listen to me. Be greedy." He leaned over and rubbed the palms of his hands firmly up her legs.

"No," she said primly, "it wouldn't be right, not with so many people about."

"They are the other side of a door through which no one would dare enter without first knocking and then awaiting my command to enter."

His hands moved up her body and drew her to him. She could no more resist the pull of his body than defy gravity.

He kissed her long and hard, until she lay beneath him, her hands around his hips, drawing him harder to him.

Then she broke away from his lips, smiling. "Not now, Zahir. Matta will be awake shortly and will join us."

As if on cue, a knock on the door was met with a brief command to enter and a sleepy Matta stumbled toward them —an innocent expecting arms to be open for him, expecting reassurance and comfort and receiving it.

With Matta stretched out half-asleep across Anna's lap, Zahir put his arms around them both and kissed her hair.

She brushed her hand against Matta's hair and turned to Zahir. "And not only bodyguards, why not give Muma Yemena a few days off, too? I know she has relations in Paris."

"So considerate of you, Anna. Nothing to do with the fact that you want him all to yourself too."

"I just want us to be together, just the three of us, like a normal family."

"Normal? What is so good about that?"

"Everything."

She closed her eyes as his hand trailed her face, around her eyes, and mouth.

"There is nothing 'normal' about you."

"Don't say that," she whispered.

She felt his lips on her eyelids, still closed so that he couldn't see the hurt that his words had caused.

"You are extraordinary in a very positive, exciting, way. Ordinary to me is something of no interest. Open your eyes."

She did. "Then perhaps we're two misfits together."

He smiled. "Perhaps."

It still hurt. She shifted away as the plane bumped twice onto the tarmac and the sound of the brakes filled the cabin, the roaring awaking Matta for a second time. She was glad of Zahir's distraction as he lifted Matta into his arms and sat him on his lap to look out the window.

She didn't want to be a misfit. She wanted to feel normal.

"So, Matta, what do you think we should do first in this beautiful city?"

Matta rubbed his eyes and peered out the window. "Don't know."

"Something very special, I think."

"Food?" suggested Anna.

Zahir laughed. "Of course. And what else, hey Matta? You remember what we talked about last night?"

Matta's eyes brightened. "Disneyworld!" he shouted.

LATER THAT AFTERNOON, with Matta nodding sleepily on top of Zahir's shoulders, they walked through the leafy streets of the Marais district, only one bodyguard following at a discreet distance. A rich light flickered through the canopy of sun-scorched leaves onto the bustle of commuters, shoppers, and people just stopping and staring at the district's beautiful historic buildings.

"So where exactly is your house?"

"I keep two homes here. One for the family is just off the Champs-Élysées and one for me." He turned to the old building facing them. "Here."

She looked up at the four-story building. "Some house."

"I wanted to be in the midst of things." Scooping Matta over his head, he held the sleeping boy in his arms and, after punching in a security code, entered the large courtyard, complete with huge tubs of orange trees. The security guard immediately entered an adjoining building, leaving the three of them alone for the first time.

Anna looked around the huge open-plan space in amazement. "Wow. I would never have believed this existed inside a seventeenth-century building."

The ostentatious seventeenth-century façade had given way to twenty-first century living inside. The black-painted wooden floors, together with the white plaster walls and minimalist furniture spoke simplicity and luxury at the same time. It was Zahir through and through.

"I had it redesigned to suit my needs."

"And you *need* a lap pool down the length of the house?" said Anna as she walked over to the glass wall that separated the pool, lit from overhead by a high, domed glass ceiling.

"Of course. I love water."

"A desert king who loves water."

"All desert kings have the greatest respect for water."

Zahir let Matta gently down onto the couch and covered him with a soft angora throw. She smiled and leaned back against the wall. She loved watching him with Matta. Once he was settled he snuggled down for a sleep, tired out from all the excitement and candy.

"Your home is beautiful."

He smiled, his lips sexily curling as he approached her and pulled off her jacket from around her shoulders.

"I like beautiful things. Particularly when pared down to their original state." He threw the jacket onto the leather couch before slipping his hands around her waist.

She wriggled away, laughing. "I have to get Matta to bed. He's exhausted. Just as well he ate well earlier. He's out for the count."

Zahir scooped him up gently. "I'll take him to bed."

Anna took a sip of her wine and watched the flames of the fire lick up the chimney, lighting stray pieces of filmy stuff that stuck to the chimney before sending them up, into the sky overhead. She'd always loved open fires and although it was still summer Zahir had indulged her.

She yawned and stretched out on the rug. She couldn't remember when she'd felt so relaxed. She smiled as she listened to Zahir say goodnight to Matta in Bedu through the intercom. It was followed by a silence in which Anna just knew that Zahir had kissed their son. She closed her eyes, feeling them prick with emotion. It was all she had ever wanted and it was all that she'd never dared dream.

Anna didn't hear Zahir re-enter the room. She didn't need to. She felt his presence as if it were something tangible like a shift in the air, a tensing in the ether. He slipped his arm around her and joined her on the floor in front of the fire.

He sighed, a deep contented sigh that said more to her than words could ever do. They were alone, with the future ahead of them, and all before them. They were so strong together. She stretched out her legs and curled them on top of his as if his body were hers. Nothing could break this bond. Nothing. She tilted her head upwards, leaning against his shoulder and heard the fire hiss as a flame worried a piece of resiny wood and the light flickered across the ceiling above.

"Thank you for today. It meant everything to me. It was just lovely."

"It was you who made it lovely. Not me. It's you who makes these things happen, makes them work, makes them complete."

The words came straight from his heart, she could feel it in the timbre of his voice and in the simplicity of his words. Whenever he said anything that was important he phrased it in the most simple terms. And that was him, she thought. Honest, upright. A "good" man all right. Someone who could be trusted with anything. Perhaps even the truth. Except he didn't want to know the truth about Abduallah.

She shifted. "Zahir. About Abduallah, I—"

He frowned. "You don't need to tell me anything. I told

you once that my memory of Abduallah, as he was and what he stood for, is important to me."

"But—"

He hushed her with his finger before it traced her lips. "But, nothing. All I need to know is here, in the lines of your body, the curve of your lips. I don't need to know anything more." He kissed her hair. "I trust you, Anna, like I've never trusted anyone before."

And she could see it in his eyes. They were naked, undefended for the first time ever. But still, deep inside of her, there was a wavering, flickering fear that refused to be extinguished.

He kissed her, stilling her mind, pushing the fear down, until she had no more thought of it. Like everything else he did, his mind was completely focused on her, his lips moved over hers with power and passion but this time with also an exquisite gentleness that was more mind-blowing than anything that went before.

She opened her mouth under his and he pulled away and touched her lips, his finger tracing around her mouth before her lips came around his finger and her tongue swept its length. She watched his eyes darken as they focused on her lips. He slowly withdrew his finger and kissed her again with the same intensity of focus but deeper, more strongly now.

Slowly he pushed the buttons of her shirt through each hole, taking time after each one, to pull the shirt open wider and drop a kiss on each newly revealed inch of skin.

He smiled, as if presented with a feast, as he pushed open the undone shirt and he descended once more, his lips trailing kisses over her stomach and up to her bra. He kissed her breasts over the bra, making no move to undo it. His tongue followed the curve of the top of the satin. Her heart thudded. His hands pinned her down so she couldn't move. It was the most exquisite torture. She wanted to respond. She tried to shift her legs, her hips, but he sat down lightly on top of her so she couldn't move. Then he very slowly unclipped her bra and gently nudged the flimsy piece of white satin aside.

Her breasts rose and fell unevenly with her jagged breathing, her pale nipples rising taut with expectation. The slow smile descended first upon one and then the other. A delicate nip and a long slow suckle before moving on to the other. The tension of his touch deepened inside her, stirring and tugging as if she were caught in a web of desire along which the slightest of movement created corresponding ripples that amplified the original stimulation.

She lifted her head to his but he merely moved back, smiling. "No, *habibti*, lay back. I want to make love to you."

She melted at his words. They'd had plenty of sex but this was the first time those words had crossed his lips. And she wanted to be made love to—more than anything. So she lay, like an adored puppet, as he pulled her strings, bringing her to life with his lips, his touch.

He shifted down, pushing away her clothes, a little more quickly now, she noticed, as his own control began to slip. And his lips descended to her thighs, caressing them with a feeling that communicated itself through every single nerve ending in her body.

She fell back into a blissful half-state of submission to the shivers of desire that ran through her body and that absorbed every thinking part of her brain. There was only sensation now, and Zahir. The two were inextricably linked. They moved as one as Zahir created magic with his mouth and tongue that, with each touch shot her further to a place that had less connection with the physical and more with the emotional.

It spiraled quickly and, as she gripped his shoulders her cries filled the room. Only then did he rise, satisfied. With his characteristic minimal, effective movement, he turned and tore off his tie and slipped off his jacket and shed the remainder of his clothes.

She watched in a heavy state of relaxation, smiling at the beauty of his body as it was slowly revealed. The width of the shoulders and the strength of the muscles beneath. His waist was no tapered youth's, but as strong and muscled as the rest of his body. It was a man's body, with its scars, muscle, and sinew. It was *her* man's body.

He turned and looked down at her and his breath caught in his chest. She was so beautiful. He pushed the palms of his hands up her legs, her thighs, her sex, her stomach, her breasts before pushing his fingers into her hair and bringing her mouth to his in a kiss that was a promise of what was to come. Then he tasted her neck, her breasts, her shoulder—stopping every few seconds to watch her skin tense with goosebumps—before moving on, burying his nose into her hair, breathing its fragrance in deep. It wasn't the perfume, the shampoo, but her. She had a freshness of purity—of newly mown grass, of a day at the beach, of the desert after a shower. He had no need to know her more than this. This was her essence.

He drew back then and knelt before her, lifting her hips so he could slip into her. With her legs wound tight around him and himself buried deep within her, he felt the familiar sensation of intense excitement as well as intense relief. He felt as if he were home. She shivered under him and dropped her head back with an echo of the same bliss that filled him.

His body responded to the stimulation of his senses as it always did with her by pushing deep within her, wanting the most intense contact possible. She wriggled around him and against him, seeking yet more stimulation, and he marveled at the slightness of her under his hands. His fingers wrapped around her hips and bottom: so slight that he felt that he filled her completely.

He felt, again, the overwhelming need to care for her, to cherish her that he'd been fighting ever since he'd learned she could not be his. He'd fought it again when she'd come to Qawaran, believing that he felt nothing other than lust that had to be satisfied. But now he felt he could no longer fight it and, for the first time, allowed himself to be swamped by his need to hold and cherish.

His hands gathered her to him and, with each movement of her own against and with his thrusting, he realized that she was as much making love to him, as he was to her. And it felt right.

His lips sought hers and they kissed a kiss that was as different from their other kisses as light from dark. There was fire still, but also a desire that was not selfish, but giving and joyful. Connected, they fell onto their sides, moving against one another, not with abandon, but with sensuous care, as one.

Slowly, very slowly their lips parted and Anna fell back on the rug. There they stayed, their eyes focused as he continued to thrust and release, as rhythmic as the ebb and flow of the constant shift of sand forming and re-forming the sand hills that rolled like waves across desert. Only after she'd cried out did he allow his own control to slip and abandon himself to the bliss of overwhelming sensation.

THEY LAY TOGETHER WATCHING darkness come in silence. Anna lay curled in his arms in a way that she'd never lain with him before. She knew something had changed for him and because of that, it had changed for her also. But she didn't dare ask, question, or try to have him explain in case it killed something of the magic she felt. She *knew* it better if it wasn't explained. Because what she knew was that they'd just made love for the first time. And things were never going to be the same again.

She wanted to hold and keep forever present the last twenty-four hours. They'd been the best in her life. She'd come to know Zahir and learn of his strengths and vulnerabilities. And it had been his vulnerabilities that had reached into her heart.

Her heart. She'd never imagined she would speak of her heart. She smiled, her lips shifting against his warm skin as they curved. Surely she hadn't imagined their closeness? He was more than wanting to ride out his passion with her, he was kind and cherishing and considerate. No, it couldn't be purely her imagination. Perhaps, just perhaps, she'd found a home with him.

CHAPTER 9

Zahir lay awake for most of the night in a state of heightened awareness. He had heard the explosion of birds that inhabited his garden and the surrounding parks and squares and had watched the pale, milky dawn light of an overcast morning find its way through the tracery of branches outside the bedroom and into the large room, shifting shadows of light and dark on the white wall.

He'd been here hundreds of times, watching the same thing but had never felt like this.

Summer madness, he thought to himself, feeling the steady beat of Anna's heart beneath his hand. Except that he knew it wouldn't pass like the seasons. Autumn would come, leaves would drop, and he would still want Anna. Winter would wreak its devastations but his passion would remain intact. And then there would be spring again, bringing with it renewal and a strengthening of all that was good.

And he knew what was good now.

He felt her stir beneath his touch. She shifted sensuously in the bed. He loved how she moved, as if her body were relishing the contact with the sheet, finding pleasure in its touch, sensitizing it ready for whatever the day would bring.

She moaned lightly and rolled toward him, nipping him playfully on the side, while moving up her head until it was next to his. She smiled.

"I was having the most amazing dream."

"About me?" he added, knowing the arrogance would amuse her.

She shook her head. "You're a lost case. No, not about you." She frowned. "Actually the absence of you." She glanced at him to make sure he wasn't offended and he schooled his face into a polite smile.

"The absence of me?" He grunted.

"I dreamed I was a qualified lawyer, traveling around the world, free to take on whatever case I wanted."

"You and your freedom, again!" He tried not to sound serious, tried to cover the wound that her words had created and from her expression it looked like he'd succeeded.

She smiled. "Yes, me and my freedom." She rolled over as if to get up from the bed but he grabbed her hand. He didn't want her to leave him, especially not with the word "freedom" on her lips. He'd have to deal with it sooner or later. But not now.

"Where do you think you're going?"

Anna laughed and fell back into bed. "To Matta. He must be awake by now."

"Let sleeping boys lie."

"It's not like him. He's usually bouncing off the walls by now."

"He's still fast asleep, or else we would have heard him on the intercom. He's tired from all the activity yesterday. He'll need to sleep."

"You mean it's convenient if he sleeps."

"As it happens, that is also true." Zahir's hand curled

around the curve of her waist, and swept lightly up her body before pulling her to him once more. "Now, where were we?"

Before Anna could remonstrate, Zahir's lips made sure she wasn't going anywhere.

It was another hour before she left to shower.

ZAHIR COULDN'T REMEMBER when he'd felt so at peace. He listened to the shower running, mingling with the rain that now angled against the window and relished the bone-deep, heavy feeling that swamped him. How had she done it? How had she got to the point where she'd captured his heart? He hadn't even seen it coming. Because there was no strategy to be aware of. Because she did it simply by virtue of being Anna: giving and generous. Tricky. He smiled. He should have known that the only way to beat him was to use methods with which he was entirely unfamiliar.

He propped himself up in bed when she emerged from the shower and watched her dress.

"Do you think this is a spectator sport?" She said without looking over her shoulder.

"Very much so. Unless you'd like to make it an audience participation sport." He started to get out of bed.

"No!" She giggled. "Get back to bed. I need to get Matta up and ready."

"I told you we should have brought his nurse."

She came and sat on the side of the bed. He pushed back a lock of her hair that fell over her shoulder. His finger caressed the bracket of her smile.

"Zahir. We are a family now. We don't need a nurse."

He hadn't thought he could feel any more than he had. But he was wrong. He pulled her to him and kissed her gently on the lips.

As he leaned back in bed again, his hand stroked down her hair, her back and lingered on her bottom.

"Then, go, get Matta ready and we will have a family day out."

She laughed. "So normal." She stood up and began to walk away. Then she glanced back with a slight frown. "You know, that was what I always wanted."

"And now? Is 'normal' enough for you or is it freedom you still crave? Freedom to be the woman you've always dreamed of being, unhindered by a demanding husband?" He covered the seriousness of his question with a smile. "Tell me Anna. Which one do you want most?"

Her frown turned into a grin. "I'm a woman, Zahir. I want everything." With that she walked out the room. She might make light of it, but he knew she spoke the truth. He felt his light dim. Perhaps he would never be enough for her to wipe out her past, to believe that they had everything together, that she didn't need to keep on looking for that elusive something that led her on and on to that goal of freedom.

∽

On the way back from lunch, Zahir and Anna lifted Matta on the count of three, swinging him between them as he squealed with delight.

The rain had diminished to a light drizzle and Matta, enjoying the memory of rainy days in New York, had insisted they walk in the rain. Laughing they came to a halt outside a brightly-lit bar.

"Look, Mom, there's Uncle James." He pointed to a tall man, with blonde carefully tousled hair and a huge, friendly grin, who was just about to enter the bar. "Uncle James!" Matta went running up to the man whose face lit up further at the sight of him.

"Mattie! Look at you! You've grown so tall. You'll be as tall as your daddy soon."

Zahir felt anger flood his body. Who was this stranger who was lifting Matta into the air? Frowning, Zahir looked at Anna who was smiling at the stranger before meeting Zahir's gaze steadily.

"Zahir." Anna walked across to Matta and the stranger. "This is James."

James kissed Anna on both cheeks and Zahir could see a true affection existed between them. Then James turned to him.

"Abdie's brother. It must be. You look so much alike."

James extended his hand which Zahir reluctantly took.

"Abduallah's brother, if that is who you mean."

Matta hung on James's arm.

James smiled, a wide disarming grin. "Sure is. And you're just like he described."

"Really." Zahir's chill response was restrained compared to the cold anger that filled his veins.

Anna looked from one to the other. "So, James, what brings you to Paris?"

"Work—and pleasure. Always pleasure." He laughed.

Zahir watched them chat easily before Anna drew it to a close after a quick look at him.

"We must go. But take care."

More kisses followed before they continued walking down the street. Zahir turned once to see James disappear into the bar—his eyes drawn to the briefly-glimpsed interior and the music thudding out into the street.

They walked in silence up the Champs-Élysées, busy traffic drowning out Matta's ceaseless conversation with Anna and her patient replies. Zahir felt himself withdraw into himself. Always his first line of defense, he knew. But for the moment the implications of what he'd just seen made it necessary.

They turned down a side street and stopped before an impressive townhouse.

"This is it?"

"Yes."

Anna's eyebrows rose. "You mean all of it?"

"Of course. My sister lives in only one wing and the rest is for visiting family."

The door swept open and they were ushered inside by a servant and shown into the elegant drawing room where Zahir's sister, Firyal—larger than life—held court surrounded by her larger than average family.

Anna watched Zahir apprehensively. He couldn't have failed to notice that Abduallah's close friend James was gay and had been entering a gay bar. But he'd made no comment. Anna settled down to listen to her sister-in-law, whom she'd only met once at the wedding, and watch their children play.

She wasn't surprised when Zahir didn't join them.

"Firyal, I must go. I have business."

Firyal nodded graciously, even though she was obviously expecting him to stay. It seemed his sisters and family all acted as if Zahir was God. No wonder he had such a shock with how Anna treated him.

"Anna." He nodded and Anna jumped up and walked with him to the door.

"Zahir, do you want to talk? Do you want to know anything?"

He shook his head. "What I want is to get away for a while."

"Shall I come? I'm sure Firyal will look after Matta."

He shook his head and pulled the door closed in front of her. There was so much she needed to tell him, so much she wanted to reassure him. But she felt helpless before his intransigence. He was a loner. Used to doing things, working things out, alone. She turned and walked back into the drawing room. She just hoped he worked things out right.

The afternoon crawled by with Anna passing the time of day with Zahir's sister—a woman with whom she had little in common except the children. Matta played and conversed easily with his cousins and aunt and her friends. She was proud of how easily he fitted in and relieved to see how his easy-going nature won people over to him. Life wouldn't be so hard for Matta as it was for his father.

Anna couldn't help gazing with increasing frequency at her watch. Hours had passed and still no sign of Zahir, no word on her phone. She knew him so well now and knew that he needed time alone. But she was also scared. What happened when the defined parameters of a strong man's world disintegrated; when a strongly held belief evaporates before your eyes? The fact that there had been no external reaction, not even a flicker of expression to reveal the turmoil that she knew to be going on within him, only concerned her more.

"Do not worry about Zahir. He is a busy man."

"I know. It's just that—"

"You worry about him? That is a woman's lot. Why don't you leave Matta with me. Let him stay the night with his friends and attend his cousin's birthday party. Then you can concentrate on Zahir."

Anna smiled in agreement. Anna couldn't say "no" even if she wanted to because she knew that Zahir needed her. Firyal didn't understand what was going on but with Matta having fun, it was true, it would give them the opportunity to have the conversation that she knew she needed to have with him. To make sure he understood fully about Abduallah.

Zahir didn't know how long he walked through the streets of Paris. His jacket collar up, slight protection against the drizzling gray rain. Once someone shouted and he looked up and stopped, just before a cab sped by in front of him. He waved in acknowledgment at the man who'd saved his life.

He raised his face to the rain, willing it to wash away the torment that had been growing in him since the first sight of Abduallah's friend James, so obviously from a world about which Zahir knew nothing: a world in which James had been intimate with Abduallah, a world from which Zahir had been excluded. Two worlds: poles apart and Abduallah had believed he couldn't belong to both. If only Zahir had known. But of course he had known—deep down—he just hadn't wanted to think about it. It didn't fit into one of his neat boxes.

He closed his eyes and slumped against a tree trunk that edged the boulevard, oblivious to curious onlookers. The wet, slippery, yet coarsely textured bark dug into his spine and he relished the discomfort. At least he could feel something other than the pain of having let his dearest brother down.

He'd failed him. He'd killed him. Anna hadn't, her family hadn't. He had.

And he would have to live with that knowledge every day of his life.

"No," the word came out like a low moan. Zahir moved away from the tree and walked toward the Pont Neuf. He gripped the damp stone as if his life depended on it watched the Seine flow slickly under the bridge, its rain-pitted surface a gray-green under the lowering sky. And he thought of his brother: his pain, his suffering and his love. He felt the cold ache of pain fill him and he hoped it would never leave.

Anna waited as darkness gathered in the empty house. It wasn't often she was alone and she felt the weightiness of the silence around her, allowing it to settle and to give her the time and peace to think.

She was afraid. How would Zahir take the discovery that Abduallah was gay? How would that affect the treasured memory Zahir had of him? Was he really as entrenched in machismo as Abduallah had believed? And what, above all else, would Zahir think of her? Married to a gay man—albeit only for a few weeks. Would he think she'd married him knowing this and wanting to be married to be part of Abduallah's wealthy family? She had no idea. All she knew was that the revelation had shaken Zahir to the core and it would have a ripple effect on everything else. She just had to wait.

She must have dozed off because when she awoke, a misty, rain-washed moon cast its weak light over her as she lay on the chaise longue before the French windows. It was late. The long dusk had faded into a dense, misty indigo light. She shifted, rubbed her eyes and wondered what had awoken her. The door closed softly and Zahir entered the room, switching on a dim lamp.

He looked exhausted, grim. He stood over her, his hair ruffled, his clothes soaking, water pooling onto the wooden floor, the drips from his sleeve forming expanding drops of darkness on the throw that covered her. She shivered and instinctively moved away. She was looking at a stranger.

"You tried to tell me didn't you?"

Even his voice sounded strange to her ears: rough, unused. She nodded but he didn't see; he turned around and repeated the question.

"You tried to tell me didn't you?"

"Yes, I tried."

"You could have tried harder, Anna."

She shook her head, injustice giving her the strength to

face this stranger. "That's not fair. I did try but you made it clear that you didn't want to hear what I had to say."

"A gay bar. A gay man. Was this man, James, my brother's lover?"

The hoarse, tortured tone in which he uttered the last few words tore at her heart. She'd never heard that tone of vulnerability in him before. It revealed a side to Zahir that had long lain hidden, she knew, even from himself and it broke down their separation. He was no longer a stranger.

"I don't think so. Closest confidante, more like. To my knowledge Abduallah was celibate. He didn't like being gay."

"Oh."

Despite the soft patter of rain that now fell, temporarily hiding the moonlight, Anna could hear a wealth of meaning in the cracked one-syllable word.

"He thought you'd be ashamed of him."

"Well I'm not. I could never be ashamed of him."

She rose and came over to him and put a hand on Zahir's arm. "Then what made him think you would be?"

Zahir shrugged. "Me, I suppose. The person I am: the fighter, the business-man, always tough, always black and white."

"Abduallah didn't know you and I don't think you even know you. That's not the person you are. Not deep down."

"And then there is our culture, our society. It is strong, but not unyielding."

"Abduallah's difficulty lay in accepting who he was, himself. He felt you wouldn't approve, he felt he wouldn't fit in, but more than that he couldn't accept his own nature. He hated himself."

"No," the moan vaguely formed the word.

"I'm sorry, but he did."

"And I thought it was you—however indirectly—that *you* and your connections were responsible for his death."

"Zahir, *I* tried to save him. I married him in ignorance and got a divorce as soon as I realized the truth. I was divorced when we came to Paris. I only came with him to see you because he pleaded with me to, because I wanted to help him. I wanted him to believe in himself. His friends, friends like James, wanted to help him. He had the choice and he chose not to live." She looked down at the rain-slicked courtyard below the window. "Not even for Matta."

Zahir turned then, his face weary, his eyes ineffably sad.

"You have it wrong, Anna. I was responsible for my brother's death. I thought you disloyal but you were being loyal to Abduallah and I thank you for that. You kept your faith with him to the end—and beyond—you even lied for him when it wasn't in your interests to do so. I thought you were the opposite of the things that I held dear, when you were in fact far more loyal than I could ever be."

"No, Zahir, that's ridiculous. You did what you could."

"But it wasn't enough was it?"

The bitterness in his tone shocked her.

Anna knelt on the bed and pressed her warm body to his wet one, trying to pull him toward her but he resisted, his eyes looking upon her with a distance that chilled her. Still she would not stop. She curled her hands firmly around resisting shoulders, her hands bunching into the damp material of his shirt.

"Zahir, stop it. Stop this. You can't do everything. You can't control everything. You can't save everyone."

He shook his head. "You don't understand. He *was* the world I was fighting for. Without that? Where is the meaning?"

"Look at your sisters, look at Matta. And Abduallah—he loved you for who you were, absolutely. So don't think your sacrifices were in vain. They weren't. They've given your family, and your people, everything. Without you, they would have nothing."

"But Abduallah would have been alive."

"You don't know that."

Suddenly the tenseness in his body slipped away as if something stern that had been holding him together had been released. She cupped his cheek, the face that was so compelling and so arrogant, now vulnerable in the extreme.

"He died because of me."

"No." She'd never seen him this desolate, this out of control. Her hands found no resistance now and she pulled him closer to her so he would have to listen, have to understand. "No, he didn't. He died because he couldn't take the hand of cards that life had dealt him."

He looked up at her with eyes that were grief-stricken. She'd never seen him like this, could never have imagined he would let anything get to him like this. He looked at her as if he hadn't heard a word she'd said, hadn't felt the touch of her hands on his body.

He closed his eyes, lost in a world of pain that he didn't want anyone else to enter. "He turned away from his family because he believed we could not understand and would condemn."

"You didn't know him but he didn't know you either." She slipped her arms around his back, weaving her fingers together, and was shocked to feel him flinch. But she refused to let him go.

"Don't try to comfort me. There is no comfort to be had."

But she would not be pushed away and she held him more tightly still.

He fought her off gently but firmly, pushing her arms away until she became furious and hit out. He caught her hand and looked down.

"I don't want your comfort. Don't you understand?"

"Tough. Because you're getting it whether you think you want it or not."

Zahir smiled then. "Remember, Matta told you not to tell me off if I've done something wrong."

"And since when do I take advice from my son?"

He shook his head. "One more thing, tell me, did Abduallah want to come home?"

It was tearing her apart seeing him so devastated but this time, whatever the consequences, she had to tell the truth.

"No. He couldn't face you."

He turned away so she couldn't see his face and blindly pulled her to him, his arm curling around her waist, drawing her into his body. And she held him like she would have held Matta when he came to her seeking comfort.

"Zahir," she said gently. "There was nothing you could have done. Abduallah was on a path to self-destruction before I met him. He was a man not happy with who he was and unwilling to face the truth about himself. Even his love for Matta couldn't save him."

He turned to her and she'd never seen his face so open, so bleak before. It was as if all life had been leached from him and he saw nothing but pain. His gaze dropped from hers and fell to her lips but he made no movement. It was up to Anna to slip her hands round the back of his head, press her fingers through his hair and pull his face down to hers. She needed to reassure, she needed to show him her love for him and, above all, she wanted to connect with him again. He felt distant and she had to bridge that distance before it became insurmountable.

His lips were cool to her own. But she held hers there, softly pressing, feeling out his with her own, insisting on a warmth of feeling that she knew to be there. But still she couldn't feel he was present. She pulled away again.

"Zahir, please."

He lifted his finger to her face and swept it across her cheek. "I've only ever seen you cry once before. When you were pleading for your son. And now?"

He looked at her with the old spark: whether it was curiosity or something else, she didn't care. She was just glad to see something.

"Now, I'm pleading for you."

He hesitated only a moment, his eyes roaming her face before he pressed his lips to hers and kissed her with all the heat and need that she could have desired. But too soon he pulled back. Silently he pushed up her sweater and pressed his cold hands against her warm stomach making her muscles clench with shock. He slid his hands under her bra and closed his eyes as his thumbs rubbed hard against her nipples. But his restless hands didn't stay there; they slid under her body and before she knew what he was doing he'd lifted her in his arms and lain her down on the bed.

She gasped as his warm lips followed his cold hands and she felt the wet heat of his mouth upon her nipples, drawing them tight until she felt the instant spiral of desire swirl inside her, obliterating all else.

Then his lips moved to hers in a kiss, so intense, that she was barely aware that he'd removed the remaining clothes that lay between them until she felt the smooth slide of him inside of her. She gasped against his lips and fell into his quickening rhythm. There was no softness, no lingering sensuous enjoyment to their love-making this time. The intensity of the kiss was reflected in the intensity in his eyes and his body. It was as if he were desperate to make that connection with her, not just on the physical level but on the emotional. They climaxed swiftly—their bodies aroused as always by each other, but their minds unwilling and unable to prolong the sensory experience.

Afterwards they lay, facing each other, holding each

other, their legs still entwined, Anna's cheek pressed against Zahir's chest, feeling his heart beat and praying that he wouldn't retreat from her, that he'd passed through the pain and could go on again, stronger than before. But he was so proud, so controlling, that she couldn't imagine what effect his newly acquired knowledge would have.

THE PAIN HURT MORE, if anything, Zahir thought, after he'd made love to Anna. It was as if he'd chosen to embrace feeling, rather than do as he'd always done, and bury it so deep that even he didn't know it was there. He looked down at her. She lay still, her cheek pressed to his chest. He knew her eyes were open, he could feel the flutter of her lashes against his chest. He understood the reason for her silence. She was giving him the only comfort she could. Herself. She was everything to him now. Everything. And the love-making they'd just had didn't show her how much he felt for her.

But he would.

CHAPTER 10

Anna scrolled down the computer screen until she came to her first university assignment results. She read it and felt the grin slowly spread across her face.

She looked up at Zahir over the breakfast table. They were sitting outside, on the rear terrace of the house, surrounded by lush green plants and tall trees reaching up into a pale blue sky. No more had been said after the previous night. Zahir's face under the soft morning sun was more open than before but what she read there didn't comfort her. He raised his eyes suddenly to hers, the frown lines deepening, while his eyes reflected back to her a little of the light of her smile.

"Good news?"

"A+!" She twisted her laptop around so he could see.

"You are surprised? I'm not."

"Relieved is what I am."

He looked at the open email on the computer screen. "And a personal note from the tutor inviting you to participate in the honors stream. We must go out and celebrate."

She shook her head, smiling. "We must stay in and celebrate."

"An excellent idea. Matta is wanting to stay another night at Firyal's so we will have the night to ourselves."

"And day."

"A day in which to make amends for my behavior last night."

She raised an eyebrow. "Your behavior? If you were bad I would have told you off. Just ask Matta."

"Not bad perhaps, but I can certainly be better and it is that I would like to show you."

"Really? Where would you like to begin?"

They held each other's gaze for a moment: hers playful, Zahir's suddenly revealing a softness she'd never seen before. He reached over and caressed her cheek with his fingers.

"Where would you like me to begin?"

She brought the palm of his hand to her lips and kissed it, before looking up flirtatiously into his eyes. "I could demand an apology, I suppose."

"You have it. I am everything you've ever accused me of: arrogant, stubborn, cold."

"True. So if you're sorry about that does that mean you're going to change?"

He sat back in his chair. "Unfortunately no. I cannot."

"Good. Because I've learned how to warm your coldness."

"Indeed you have."

"And I know how to get through to your stubbornness."

He frowned. "Stubborn is simply another word for sticking to one's beliefs."

"Yes and I know it's hard for you to understand but sometimes, just sometimes, you're wrong. And sticking to what you believe in when you're wrong, is just plain dumb."

"I am always open to rational argument."

"Just as well I'm going to be a hot-shot lawyer then, isn't

it?" She grinned. "So that just leaves your bossy, arrogant ways. And you don't have to apologize for them either because I'd kind of miss them if they went away. I mean, where would the fun be in disregarding a bossy man?"

"You dare disregard me?"

"Of course. And where would be the thrill in teasing a humble man?"

"Fun and thrills. Is that all you are after from me?"

His brown eyes had warmed and formed the hot connection she'd been seeking. A slow smile spread over her lips as she slipped off her sandal and lifted her foot under the table and swept the arch of her foot up his calf, his thighs, before she found her target and caressed him intimately. His eyes flicked closed momentarily as he felt the smooth caress of her foot, arched to cup him with her toes molding to fit his hardening shape.

"Exactly."

"Come here." His voice was gruff, hoarsely aroused.

"There you are again, being bossy." Her foot didn't stop moving. "I told you I don't respond to bossy men."

"You respond well to me, at night, in the dark. You recognize the truth of my words then. Perhaps I need to show you why you need to come to me now."

He caught hold of her foot and rubbed his thumb up its length, touching enough pressure points to ignite several parts of her body at once. With her foot resting once more on his lap where it resumed its caress, his hands swept up her bare leg briefly tracing the moist curves of her sex over her panties before dragging his nails down her leg again.

He took her foot and let it drop to the ground.

"Come here," he repeated.

She had no choice but to go. "It's only because I want to," she said defensively as she sat down on his lap. "You can be very persuasive." He pulled her face to his in a kiss that made her forget what she was being defensive about. She pushed her hands under his shirt, wanting to feel more of him, needing his clothes to be gone. She pulled away from his lips and stood up, relishing the look on his face of unabashed lust as she stripped off her panties. She unzipped his trousers carefully until she could hold him in her hands as she straddled him, skimming the surface of his arousal with her own.

"Woman. You're teasing me."

"As I said, I like to tease."

Two strong hands pulled her down on him and all teasing ceased.

He knew what she was doing but he had no wish to stop. It was too pleasurable even if it was ineffective. The morning had passed in passionate love-making outside in the bijoux garden overlooked by nothing but the birds, trees, and sky. He'd made use of the softly springy, pungent chamomile on which to lay the tender, pale body of his lover—the only lover he would ever have in the true sense of the word, he now knew. He watched her skin peak under the chill of the light breeze and flush under the internal fire that his thrusting ignited, and all the while felt himself sinking deeper into this woman who had changed his life. It was only when the pale blue sky had turned to gray and they'd lain, hearts beating, soft rain coating their sweat-slicked bodies, that he felt her begin to chill and he carried her upstairs to the bed.

He didn't make love to her again immediately but simply took time to indulge himself in the pleasure of looking at Anna's beauty: her cool, blond hair, blonder where the harsh desert sun had caught the top-most strands, more golden beneath. Fine hair, that poured like silk over the pillow and his muscled, brown forearm. He loved watching her pleasure: it wasn't superficial, but a deeply felt thing that took its time forming and took its time dissipating. He loved watching her and absorbing the fact that somehow she had come to mean more to him than he did himself.

Strangely the thought didn't appall him, it was so right. She completed him in a way that he didn't even know was necessary. The only thing that appalled him was how he'd used her: the angry, bitter things he'd said to her when he'd believed she was not only married to his brother but, later, pregnant with his child; the force with which he'd coerced her into marrying him; the way he'd trapped this beautiful, free woman who didn't ever deserve to be trapped again.

He lay alongside her but not touching her for a long time. Her eyes fluttered from time to time and drifted into a light sleep before awaking with that slow, pleasurable stretching of the limbs, the same sensuous pleasure gained from the feel of the fine cotton sheets against her body. Then she'd turn, knowing he was there, aware that he was still watching her but totally unselfconscious, she'd return his gaze.

Only then did he reach out for her. He needed to know her—every part of her, needed to press it into his memory. His hand hesitated briefly before his fingers pressed lightly to her temples before brushing down her face, her neck. There he stayed, fascinated by the solid push of skin containing her pulse—the beat of her heart. But he couldn't touch that tiny patch of skin—it held too much that he wanted. It put fear into his heart because it seemed so fragile a thing to contain so much life.

Then her hand came over his and wove her fingers into his and pushed them high above them together, a union of flesh, bone, and sinew in the soft light of the drizzly afternoon. She twisted their hands first one way and then the other. His dark brown skin a stark contrast to her moon-white flesh; his large, muscled fingers and hand obedient to the sway and pull of her slender white fingers.

Then she pulled their hands to her lips and closed her eyes and kissed their joint fists. She opened her eyes and continued to gaze at their hands as tightly entwined as a heart.

"Something's changed."

Her words were so soft they seemed to come from an echo of his own thoughts. When she looked at him he realized the words were hers. He nodded.

"Yes."

"Tell me."

"I can't. You won't like it."

"That's never stopped you telling me things before. Try me."

How could he put into words how much she was to him now, how he felt their lives and souls were entwined in a way that he knew would be repugnant to the woman who had always stated that her one desire was to live independently of people, of family, to be free? It would be the one thing that would drive her away. And he could never use force to keep her again.

"I'll show you instead."

She'd never before heard his voice so tender, never felt his touch so tentative as if exploring the unknown. Whether he was unsure of her reaction or of his own, she didn't know. All she knew for certain was that something had definitely changed within him.

She knew that he felt responsible for his brother's death, guilty that his harsh world-view had trapped his brother in a life from which he could have rescued him, if he'd only been more open. It was as if the knowledge had crack the tough outer shell with which Zahir faced the world.

He held himself above her and kissed her lingeringly on

the lips. His knees positioned between hers, wedging open her legs, she felt the pulse of her body there, as he kissed the pulse in her neck and then down further. He cupped each hand under her breasts and suckled each nipple in turn until he was satisfied. But she wasn't. She moaned and lifted up her hips to wrap her legs around his. But he wasn't ready yet. He smiled and shook his head as he dipped his mouth to kiss her lower, much lower, sucking and nipping her sensitive skin and tasting her arousal until she shook and cried out his name.

It was her turn now and she swiftly slid down the bed and took him fully into her mouth, wanting to taste him as he had tasted her. She felt his buttocks clench under her hands as she pulled and sucked him into her mouth, loving the feel of his shaft against her lips, loving the taste of him against her tongue, and loving the fact that his control was finally breaking down.

She pulled her mouth away and looked at the end of his dark shaft upon which a drop hung, suspended, a jewel for her alone. Her body shook with need and his, too, was trembling now. His hands lowered to come around her bottom and lift her up so that he could enter her but she stopped him, her focus entirely on that drop. Slowly, so slowly she extended her tongue and lapped at the end of his shaft: that drop slipping down her throat like the most exquisite liqueur.

He groaned and pushed her back, her bent legs flat against her body as he entered her up to the hilt with one swift movement. There was no hesitation now. He pumped into her, not waiting for her reaction but in the moment with her and they came together for the first time, Zahir crying out Anna's name loudly in relief as if he'd lost her and only just found her.

IT WAS LATE by the time Anna awoke. She'd been dreaming of the desert—its wide, open spaces, its shimmering heat and the palace built into the side of the mountain, solid and dominating. She had a residual feeling of peace and sighed, her eyes opening to the soft mellow of the Parisian sunset. The sense of peace deserted her immediately as it became replaced by panic. She'd felt happy, easy, at home in her dream. Her heart beat quickly. She could never feel at home there because it wasn't her home. She looked over at Zahir who lay beside her. Unusually for him, he was quite still, looking up into the flickering pink light of the low sunlight filtering through the leaves. Qawaran was Zahir's home and hers only for as long as he wanted her there. She had to remember that and usually, during the day, she did. It was only in her dreams that feelings of security crept up on her.

Suddenly a sense of panic gripped her. Something had happened in his mind. She knew it had. It had begun with the discovery of his brother being gay and it had ended with their love-making. It had a different quality about it that day: a sadness, a sense almost of desperation, of taking the moment rather than observing the moment. With vivid clarity Anna suddenly saw that it had ended. Zahir had finally worked through his need for her. That's why the urgency had gone; that's why he was quieted. She was no longer required.

She lay there in shock, not wanting to move, not wanting to prompt him into action, into speech that would reinforce her fears.

She almost flinched when his hand reached over for hers and gripped it tight in a fist before releasing it. She jumped up and collected her clothes.

"Where are you going?"

She shook her head—unwilling to talk, to confront what she knew to be true—and got dressed.

"Where are you going?" he repeated.

"Just out for a walk."

Zahir opened his mouth to speak—whether to ask further questions, whether to suggest he accompany her—she didn't know because he closed his mouth before saying anything. Further proof that he didn't want her.

She instinctively stepped away from him. She couldn't bear to see the indifference on his face anymore and left the room before she made more of a fool of herself than she already had.

She wasn't gone long. Just long enough for him to pack his things, ready for the morning, and fall back into bed. He felt tired, more tired than he had ever felt before, even when his muscles were screaming after days of forced marching across the parched desert. Then he'd felt a purpose. Now, he felt nothing. Only emptiness.

She'd recoiled from him as if she thought he was trying to contain her, hold her against his will. Well, wasn't that precisely what had happened? He'd taken her liberty—the one thing she wanted—and she'd left because she needed to regain that space. She'd always told him that, always stated the facts of her dreams baldly. And the facts were now plain. He loved her. She wanted to be free. So, he would give her freedom to her.

The door banged closed behind her, driven by the wind. He smiled. Anna couldn't come or go anywhere incognito, quietly. He heard her hesitate in the sitting room, heard the skid of her handbag as she threw it untidily onto the floor, and the sound of her weary footsteps approaching.

Believing him to be asleep she slipped off her clothes and crept into bed beside him. There was nothing but the chill summer night air blowing out the pale curtains and the tick of his alarm clock beside him. It showed him it was three in the morning. Where had she been? He didn't know and now knew that it was none of his business.

He didn't know how long he lay, watching her, watching the city lights flicker through the trees. Outside, Paris was rain-washed, like a water-color painting. Like a painting from the note-book that he'd discovered in the night, while she was away. Small, primitive water-color paintings of scenes of the desert, of Matta and of a bird in flight. The falcon—his falcon—was portrayed both in mid-flight, wings flexed against the turbulent air currents that played above the desert, and captured with its hood on. The colors downplayed in the latter, that was also a study of a hand, dark, strong, and weathered. His hand. It didn't take a genius to see her desires and fears made manifest in those pictures.

Sleeping on her front, her hair over her flushed cheek, one hand flat against the bed, still warm from his body. The covers were pushed down revealing the pale curves of her shoulder blades and her spine dipping down into the small of her back. Her face wasn't peaceful in this sleep. Her eyelids flickered as she watched unknown scenes unfold inside her head—scenes that he would never know, but could guess at. He turned from her face, needing respite from the regret that ate him up, and looked out the window down which rain ran in trickles, distorting the world; turning it into a place that was crazed, cracked, like the egg-shell varnish on a masterpiece painting. His need for control had always tainted everything he'd done and everything he'd said. But now nothing was under control; nothing was whole.

He'd seen Anna as someone who threatened to fracture his world and so dealt with her in the only way he could: took her and made her his. Except it hadn't worked. Instead she'd shattered his control from the inside.

He gently pushed her hair back from her face. She stirred slightly, then settled and went back to sleep.

Warmth flooded him and he reached out for her, but he stopped himself before he could touch her. It was a warmth that filled him and obliterated any need for control: it controlled him and he didn't care anymore. There was a sense of relief, a shaking out of priorities. Things suddenly seemed extremely simple.

He moved away from her.

So simple now. There was nothing more important than her and what she needed and wanted. And he knew what that was. She'd never made any attempt to hide it. She'd always wanted her freedom: to be who she could be, not who everyone expected her to be.

There was only one thing he could give her now, and that was her independence.

He lay waiting for her to awake. His eyes felt hot from watching, imprinting into his mind her beauty, imprinting into his mind the woman he loved.

Hours drifted past while his mind raced and he listened to her twist and turn; the times when her breathing was disturbed followed swiftly by the deep breathing of sleep. It was only when dawn was beginning that she reached across the cold divide between them and gently stroked his face, stopping short of his eyes.

"You're crying." Her surprise made the words light and hazy.

He pressed his eyes tight close. "No, I'm not."

"Then what do you call water that falls from the eyes? Not *ma-ush-shafa*, not healing water?"

"No. The opposite."

She kissed first one closed eye and then the other with a tenderness that made his heart ache.

"Open your eyes."

He didn't immediately. But when he did, he covered her hand with his and pulled it down from his face.

"What is it?"

He shook his head and rolled out of bed, his head in his hands for a few seconds before he rose and began to dress.

"It's early. Where are you going?" Her voice was faint as if from miles away. The distance made it easier to do what he needed to do.

"Away. Back to Qawaran."

"But I haven't finished my work here. A few more days at least. And Matta?"

"I'm going alone. You stay. Matta can stay for another week and then he will need to return to me. He may return to you later."

She threw off the bedclothes and leaped out of bed naked and seething. She gripped his shirt with a fist and shook her hand, her eyes blazing.

"So that's it. You've had enough? Well what if I haven't?"

He was pleased. He barely felt the anger of her spirit and the tumult of her emotions screaming at him. He could barely feel it because they were nothing beside the pain of his own.

"You will have what you've always wanted, your freedom."

He didn't turn around again. He couldn't. It might have threatened his resolve. He needed to give her what she wanted. Without that she would always resent him. The door banged shut behind him closing off a part of him forever.

CHAPTER 11

The long days of willing the cellphone to ring had turned into weeks and then months where her only respite was her studies. But the pain hadn't ebbed at all; it had grown if anything—this missing him, this aching.

From her desk she'd watched the green leaves of summer turn into the rich flood of autumn leaves. The summer semester had come and gone and Matta was returning from Qawaran in a week, to start his new school in Paris. And still no word directly from Zahir until now—until the papers that made legal his generosity had arrived—the same day she received confirmation of her exam results.

She looked down at the piece of paper that confirmed her results and felt—nothing. She wanted to share it with someone but there was no one. Impulsively she dialed Zahir's number on her cellphone but it reverted to his assistant immediately. It always did.

She switched off her cellphone and flung it across the sofa. He had gone and he wouldn't even take any of her calls. She sat stiffly, her arms crossed, staring, unseeing across the room.

He'd told her he was giving her her freedom and he had. She looked down with distaste at the papers he'd had sent through to her, strewn across the coffee table: deeds to the Paris house—hers; huge monthly income—hers. She had everything she could want. She looked around at the luxurious house—of the best quality but so simple and honest in its design, so Zahir. She had everything. She had nothing.

He'd gone forever.

She repeated the words to herself. Trying to make herself believe them. But she couldn't. How could so much disappear into nothing? A conjuring trick, magic, maybe. It wasn't real. It couldn't be real. Like a mirage of water on a hot, dry desert, perhaps it was a trick of the light, an imagining that would disappear in time, with nothing greater than a change of light? But she sat watching dust motes barely move in the quiet of the room, watching the late sun slant mellow beams of light over the floor and feeling the quiet emptiness of the place that she knew wasn't going to change. Because it wasn't only external; the emptiness also lay within.

She walked over to fridge and plucked out a bottle of champagne—the one she'd chosen to celebrate her exams with Zahir, still imagining that he'd show up. But he wasn't here was he? It was just her. And she had more to celebrate than her exams. She had her independence that Zahir had given her.

She popped the cork and poured herself a glass. So tense she was nearly shaking, she watched with exaggerated concentration the pale gold liquid effervesce in her glass, as she remembered Zahir's last cold exchange with her. She didn't notice the glass was full and didn't stop pouring until it was too late. And even then she didn't care. Simply watched as it flowed over the glass and pooled onto the highly polished wood of the table. What did it matter? She stopped pouring though and just stared at it and swallowed hard and took a deep breath. Of course it mattered.

She swung around and held up the glass to no one.

"To me and my success."

But she didn't drink. You didn't drink when you were pregnant—bad for the child. That's what everyone said.

She felt a wave of nausea overwhelm her at the smell of the alcohol and only just made it into the bathroom in time. Hands still clenching the sides of the bowl, she looked up into the mirror at a face pale, drained, eyes darkly shadowed and lifeless despite the extra life within her.

Who would want her now, looking like this? She'd lost weight again and she knew Zahir liked curves on a woman. Perhaps she'd already been replaced by a woman more curvaceous, less demanding, easier to fit within the strict parameters of his cut and dry life.

Then the fears that had been lurking at the back of her mind surfaced loud and clear.

He might not want you but he will want your baby.

He could want all he liked. He'd never find out. She wasn't showing much and she'd have to make excuses to Matta for the last few months to stop the cuddles. But she could arrange for him to be in Qawaran during the last few months. Thank God for the Qawaranian robes she still wore. They hid everything. And when the baby was born? She couldn't even think that far ahead.

She wandered back to the table and flicked the deeds to the house open with the bottom of the glass. Champagne had spilled into the paper, its stain spreading through the expensively textured paper.

"I have everything I've ever wanted," she whispered. "Everything I ever told Zahir I wanted he's given to me now."

The silence within the house contrasted to the shouts of children in the square gardens below.

She turned—tension, anger and frustration merging into one—and threw her glass against the marble fireplace. It splintered into hundreds of pieces, shattering and skittering across the hard, wooden floor.

"Everything!" she shouted. "He's given me everything except what I wanted all along."

She jumped up suddenly and tried to warm the chill that seemed to be seeping into her; frantically she rubbed her arms up and down, trying to stimulate the circulation that appeared to have gone into shock.

"No. It's okay." She paced. "I wanted freedom. I've got freedom." She stopped, suddenly realizing what exactly freedom meant. "I've got freedom from everything. I'm cut off, alone." She sat down and put her head in her hands. She groaned. She'd never meant that to happen, had never imagined for one minute that she'd actually want to keep her connection with someone.

But he didn't want to keep it with her. Zahir had done what he'd always set out to do, rid himself of his obsession with her and now he, too, was free. And he'd made the most of it. Hadn't hung around to celebrate their mutual freedom, but had left as soon as he could.

It was hours before Anna moved, could even think clearly enough through her grief to realize where she was or what she should do. It was only when the street lamps outside flicked on that she realized she'd sat in the same position the whole evening through.

Stiffly she rose and looked around. She cleaned up the mess of the stale alcohol and slipped on her warm robes. Somehow, wearing them, she felt closer to Zahir, more comfortable, more herself. She went to the telephone and dialed Qawaran. This time she wanted to speak to her son.

But Matta wasn't available—he was out in the desert on a hunting party expedition with Zahir. She smiled. She knew he would enjoy it. And she would be seeing him soon there. Zahir had given her joint custody and allowed her free access. She was scheduled to go to Qawaran at the end of the month to collect Matta and bring him back to begin the autumn term in Paris. But she knew full well that Zahir would not be seeing her again. He'd finished with her. He'd never promised her anything other than a brief time together. But, oh, how she'd believed differently.

She rarely cried. Zahir had noticed. She'd cried when she pleaded for Matta; she'd cried when she'd pleaded with Zahir and she cried now, for herself. For her lost self, alone in her world of freedom. It wasn't capture she'd been avoiding after all, it had been a home she was seeking: an emotional one—one that came with people who loved her and a place where she felt safe. She'd found it and somehow she'd let it slip through her fingers.

She jumped up and faced herself in the mirror. She saw a fierce look in her eyes, one of a warrior—a desert warrior—who wasn't going to sit back and let her man leave without a fight. She'd stick to Zahir's beloved schedule for Matta's sake but she would make sure she saw Zahir in Qawaran. Somehow.

~

SHE TOOK A DEEP BREATH. Oh, how she'd missed the smell of the desert—dusty yet clean—and the sounds of the desert—the clatter of date palms and birdsong, the sounds and smells of freedom. She'd spent time with Matta who was looking forward—a little scared and a little excited—to starting his new school in Paris. But she hadn't seen Zahir who was always busy, unable to be disturbed. Zahir might be determined not to see her. But he'd underestimated her determination to see him.

She hated the falconry with its mesh of cages, its hooded birds. It was everything that scared her: the bird's sharp talons flexing on their perches, the mute shuffle of their feet, the hint of power still in their feathers now sleek and unruffled. Waiting. Simply waiting until they were allowed to fly. Zahir would never expect her to be there. Therefore, there she must be.

He looked exactly the same. She hadn't expected that. When she looked in the mirror she saw a changed woman. But Zahir, despite the self-recriminations and blame he'd loaded onto himself over Abduallah's death, looked exactly the same. He'd grown hard again. Still, even if it ended in failure she had to tell him something that she'd never expressed to him before.

"Zahir!" Her voice was soft but she knew he'd heard because his shoulders froze. He didn't turn round.

She walked up to him and first looked at his face, his eyes narrowed as they stared into the bright sunlight of the desert. He didn't look down at her, nor make any indication that he knew she was there. So she followed his gaze to his falcon, circling overhead.

"Aren't you going to speak to me?"

"What is there to speak about? I assumed you've come to see Matta not me. In which case you've come to the wrong place. He will be in the school room at this hour."

"I know. I've just come from there."

"And you found everything satisfactory? He is sufficiently prepared to begin his new school?"

She nodded, not knowing whether to laugh or cry at his coldness. "Yes. Everything is satisfactory. Matta is happy and well and keen to get started in Paris."

He held up his gloved hand to the hawk. "Good."

The bird landed on his arm, the breeze of his passage blew Anna's hair back it was so strong. She took a deep breath while she admired the bird. The same bird that months ago she would not go near.

"May I?" For the first time Zahir glanced at her but she could read nothing in his black eyes. Coolly, he nodded.

She reached up and tentatively stroked the feathers of the bird. They were not soft but held the tensile strength of a fine fabric designed for hard wear. Deceptive.

"He's beautiful."

"He's a wild thing made tame. I no longer know if that's a beautiful thing."

She touched his arm then, insisting that he meet her gaze. "You can't release him back to the wild."

"No. It's too late for that."

She stroked the bird but kept her hand firm on Zahir's arm. "He's known your touch and will always crave it."

Zahir abruptly dropped the hood onto the bird's head and the bird immediately relaxed and his head sunk down into his body.

"Captive once more." He turned to face her, his arm and the bird outstretched to the side.

She shook her head, absorbed in the beauty of Zahir's face and body. He was as rugged as the land and as dignified and upright as his people. The wind stirred his headdress, the only thing that moved around a face that was hard and set. She turned away and looked out at the flat plains that stretched forever and wondered how she could have ever longed for what lay beyond them when what she'd wanted had been before her all the time. But, judging by his unmoving expression, she wondered if it was too late.

"Captive, or perhaps simply home now?"

His eyes narrowed further.

"Why are you here?"

"I told you—to collect Matta."

"No here, in the falconry. You have no further business with me. I thought I made that plain."

Shock slammed into her gut and she stumbled back as if physically struck and turned away, suddenly realizing she'd made a huge mistake by coming to see him. But the pain in her heart, that she rubbed instinctively, told her otherwise. Whatever he felt, she simply had to know for sure because she couldn't go on without knowing. She turned back to face him.

"That was the only thing you made plain. Nothing is ever so black and white as you want to believe."

He shrugged. "People over-complicate things. With us, it was simple. I never made false promises to you. We had a deal: I wanted you until I grew bored and you wanted your freedom. Well, that is what happened. And it *did* have to happen." He added more quietly.

The remaining shreds of Anna's strength dissolved with that final blow. She'd trusted her emotions in returning to him and she'd been wrong. She couldn't believe that everything they'd had had come to this. But apparently it did. Zahir didn't love her after all.

"I'm sorry. I—"

"I think you should go, don't you? Return to Matta and then at the end of the week return to Paris as planned."

"As planned," she muttered under her breath. "So that's it. I won't be seeing you again."

"While you are here of course you must join us for dinner."

His cold civility was worse than any abuse. She was a stranger to him now and he couldn't have made it plainer.

"Of course. I couldn't think of anything nicer." Two could play at that game.

He passed his falcon to a keeper to return her to the

falconry and walked back with her to the palace. "I trust your studies are going well."

"Of course. It's all going to plan. Studying full time I should be complete my first year in six months."

"And then you will have everything you've always wanted."

She stopped. "No. No I won't." They had stopped in the public foyer of the palace and a sweep of cars suddenly entered the courtyard outside.

"I'm sorry, Anna. Let me know what it is you are lacking and I will have someone take care of it for you."

"It's not something someone can take care of. You can't delegate this. I need to tell you something, Zahir. We need to talk."

"Not now. I have business to take care of. I will see you at dinner." He nodded formally and turned away, all thought of her apparently forgotten.

She backed away, unable to tear herself away from him completely. She stopped in the shadows of the palace and studied his face. She wanted to remember every nuance of shade, every line etched by experience, pain and sadness and happiness on that face. She wanted to feed her soul on him because she knew her time with him was limited. She realized this might be the last time she ever saw him.

She watched as he greeted the small family group that emerged from the convoy of cars, bringing forth a gorgeous dark-eyed, dark-skinned young woman. It was obvious by the body language of all concerned that the woman was being offered to Zahir.

Anna couldn't watch anymore but turned and tried to walk without stumbling across the uneven paving of one of the older, disused paths around the palace, taking her away from Zahir and his guests. She felt numb, barely felt the sharp edges of the crumbling stone beneath her thin sandals or the blazing sun on her head. It was as if she had no physical substance, only deep, unadulterated grief. Somehow she made it back to her room. There, she slammed the door shut and concentrated on breathing, on slowing down the heart that threatened to burst from her chest.

∽

"Are you coming to dinner then?"

Anna looked up from the sketch book she'd been doodling in, surprised at Matta's question.

Matta lay on his stomach on the floor coloring in. He didn't stop the heavy pressure of his pencil on the paper shifting jaggedly up and down, to speak to her. He seemed to be able to focus better on a conversation if he was busy with something else at the same time. Anna wished she had that ability. At the moment all she could do was to lie stretched out on a couch, a fan strategically placed beside her trying to keep at bay the heat, sickness, and exhaustion.

"No, I don't think so, darling, I'm feeling tired."

"Muma Yemena didn't think you would be."

"And why's that?"

"Because of our guests." Matta suddenly stopped working on his picture and flicked her a deep, yet concerned look. "Because of the lady who is staying here."

She felt a chill run in her veins. "Ab Zahir said it was business."

"People say that Ab Zahir needs a new lady as you're in Paris all the time."

Anna could hardly speak but she had to, to make sure Matta understood. She rose and put her arms around him, holding back the stinging tears that threatened. "You mustn't listen to what people say. It's just gossip. And whatever Ab Zahir decides to do, don't worry. He and I love you and will always love you. Nothing he does will ever make any difference to that."

"Mom, it's not just me; I'm worried about you."

She could hardly breathe with love and grief. "But you mustn't worry about me."

"And I do worry about me too. You used to love Ab Zahir like you love me. And now you don't. Perhaps you might not love me any more soon if I'm naughty?"

"I will always love you. And I will always love him."

"For real? How much do you love Ab Zahir?"

It was killing her telling her young son these things but she had no alternative but to reveal to him her deepest feelings if she were to reassure him.

"You remember that story I used to read to you about the hare that loved his baby over the moon and back?"

He was silent for a moment and Anna watched with an aching heart as he riffled through his selection of coloring pencils and selected one, his brow contracting with concentration, whether on her words or his drawing, she didn't know. "I've never seen a hare."

"Well, you know when you lose sight of the falcon and you think he's gone out beyond where you can understand? You think he's lost but he's not?"

"Yeah."

"Well I love your Ab Zahir beyond where I can see, beyond what I know."

"Way beyond a falcon can fly? Wow. That's a long way."

"Yes. I suppose it is." Satisfied with the answer Matta immediately continued where he left off, coloring in an outline of a falcon. Matta's tongue peeped out from between lips pursed in concentration. Her heart swelled. She loved everything little thing about Matta. And she missed him desperately when she was gone. But there was nothing she could do about that. This was his world, not hers anymore.

But he would be returning to Paris soon. He would have two worlds. The best of two worlds, she reminded herself.

"Do you like it, Mom?" He held up the half-completed picture where the initial hard-pressed lines of careful color had given way to broad, swift strokes that went beyond the outline of the bird. It was an illustration of impatience. That was something he'd inherited from her.

"The colors are exactly right and you've caught the energy of the bird with those swift strokes."

He looked at it critically. "Ab Zahir said I need to keep within the lines. But it's hard."

"Yes, it's hard all right." And trust Zahir. Matta was already fidgeting, wanting to get on to the next thing, watching his friends playing with a ball out in the courtyard.

"Can I go, Mom?"

"Wait, one moment." She caught hold of him to keep him from wriggling away. "Remember tomorrow I will go and you will follow me in a few weeks. But you will see your friends at the end of term. Not long. And you will make lots of new friends in Paris. And your other cousins will be there."

"Yeah."

"And we have a few days before school starts. How about another trip to Disneyworld?"

"Cool. Can I bring some friends?"

"Of course you can. Just clear it with Ab Zahir first."

A blur of hugging and kissing and then he was gone in a haze of dust. She watched the piece of coloring drift down onto the marble floor.

Yes, she did love Zahir, further than the falcon could fly. But she would not be going to dinner, would not be saying good-bye to him. She couldn't stand to see him looking at another woman as he'd once looked at her.

CHAPTER 12

Zahir watched the dust billow and settle from the trail of vehicles that marked the end of the visit from distant relatives and the lovely Aisha. Despite his firm denials of interest his family had encouraged their visit and it had ended, predictably, in disaster. They meant well and he'd never met anyone more beautiful than the young woman, or anyone who left him more cold.

All through the interminable dinner he'd sat surrounded by talk that he couldn't bear to listen to. His thoughts were of a woman who was as prickly as Aisha was placid; as feisty as Aisha was submissive and as complex as Aisha was straightforward. He should want Aisha. Any sensible man would. But, instead, his mind was focused on a woman who played his body and mind like a virtuoso, creating a magic that he found he craved more with each passing day.

But what could he—a destroyer of love and life—possibly give to anyone? Especially someone like Anna? He'd given her the only thing she wanted and the only thing he could give her. She'd never told him she loved him, never said she wanted anything different to her dreams of freedom.

And, despite specifically asking her to dine with them, Anna hadn't joined them in the dining hall that had been full of people and laughter but had felt empty without her. The thought suddenly occurred to him that she might have listened to gossip about his visitor. But he dismissed it. Anna wasn't the type to believe gossip. No, she was the type to do as she pleased. She'd fought for the freedom to do just that and she'd won it. She hadn't come to dinner because she simply hadn't wanted to dine with him. The conversation she claimed she wanted to have with him obviously wasn't pressing. It couldn't have been as important as preparing for her return trip to Paris. She'd left at first light, leaving a message that she needed to do some shopping in Riyadh and would meet Matta there before going on to Paris. And she disappeared without trying to see Zahir again.

"Ab Zahir! Look."

Zahir turned to his son, a welcome diversion from the pain he felt at his loss, a distraction that numbed the pain into a dull heaviness from which he could never escape.

Matta held out his arm, steady and strong, with the small hawk perched on top. The pride on the boy's face at his achievement reminded him of Anna. The set of the face was the same: determination and courage despite a sensitive nature. If Matta looked like him physically, he was proud to see that he possessed his mother's charm and essentially happy nature. He was someone who showed exactly what he was thinking and feeling in his expressive body and face.

"Excellent, but be sure to be steady for her. Any nervousness or doubt will betray itself in your arm and she will become agitated."

"I'm strong, Ab Zahir. Mom says so. It will be fine. How far will she fly?"

"She is young and not so strong as the peregrine."

Matta was absorbed in the bird, watching each movement

of its eyes, every flicker of its feathers. "Not as far as Mom's love for you then."

Zahir froze. "What did you say?"

Matta held up his bird aloft, shifting it in the light still distracted and absorbed by its beauty and the sense of ownership. "Nothing."

"You said something about your mom. Matta, tell me."

Zahir's sense of urgency got through to Matta who turned his head to Zahir. "Nothing much. Just that Mom said she loved you beyond where we could see the falcon fly. That's big isn't it?"

Zahir followed Matta's gaze to the distant horizon. It *was* big. It was also impossible. Perhaps Matta had misheard. But no, it wasn't the kind of thing the boy would invent. The falcon could fly forever, find its freedom anywhere.

For the first time in months the heaviness that weighed him down lifted and he felt light with possibility. Swiftly followed by doubt. Was her love big enough to encompass his shortcomings? The extreme swoops of doubt and happiness echoed the uncertain, erratic movements of Matta's young hawk taking its first flight. It was the complete opposite of how Zahir liked to be. It was out of control, erratic. But that wasn't life, was it? He'd learned that through letting Abduallah down. If there was the remotest possibility that Anna might want him then he needed to know. And there was only one way to find out.

~

THE WIND WHIPPED AWAY the leaves that were only just turning brown, tearing them prematurely from their precarious hold. Paris was alive with the roaring of the wind and the slapping of rain on her window. Each day passed more slowly than the last as the world abruptly turned into an autumn that Anna couldn't consider yet. Her mind seemed to have slipped into some kind of stasis, unable to move on and unable to let go of the life that summer had brought.

But she had to. Zahir was moving on with his life and so must she. She sighed and re-read the letter from Zahir's solicitor that she'd received. She'd been sorting out her papers rather than gaze at the ravaged trees that twisted and turned in the blustery wind outside her window, but kept coming back to the letter. It had asked her to attend a meeting. About what, it didn't say. But there was only one thing it could mean. Zahir wanted a divorce. She couldn't face it. Her morning sickness was worsening rather than improving. It looked like she'd be ill the whole nine months, just as she had been with Matta. But what she really couldn't take was the finality of the end of their relationship. She couldn't bear to discover he was going to marry someone else. She didn't think she could go on if he was.

So she'd missed the meeting that she should have attended that morning and had stayed, instead, determined to clear through the mass of papers that she'd somehow accumulated. She forced herself to read through another paper before dropping it in the bin. Then another and then her mind drifted back to the tossing trees and the leaden sky, imagining it as the desert sky: so big and brilliant. She snapped out of her reverie and continued to sort through her papers, wondering how she could have found the strength to study as hard as she had.

She sat back heavily in her chair and sighed. Truth was, it was a Godsend that she had something to distract her from the man who had stolen her heart and left her a few precious memories. Her hand moved to her stomach and a sense of deep sadness swept her, swiftly followed by anger. She tossed all the papers into a basket. She'd continue with her studies but they were no longer her life. They'd only been her life when she had no love in it. But now she had experienced love, everything else was secondary.

Since her return to Paris life had resumed some sort of normalcy. This was where she lived now. It wasn't her home, it would never be her home, but was simply a place where she lived. Matta went to school, albeit an exclusive one where he rubbed shoulders with the rich and the royal and had already settled well after one short week. He missed Zahir but Zahir had promised Matta he would visit him soon. To see only Matta, thought Anna ruefully.

She'd tried to discover more about Zahir from Matta, tried to weave into their talk and play anything that would reveal what Zahir felt for her. But it seemed there was nothing to say. Zahir kept his feelings close to his chest, as always. All she knew was that the lady had gone home, and he hadn't yet sought divorce proceedings. Nor had she. But times had changed and it appeared he wanted to move on. Well he'd have to move on without help from her. Was there someone else like he'd implied? Was it the young woman whom she'd seen at the palace only a few weeks ago?

If Matta knew he wasn't telling.

She looked at her watch. One of Zahir's men should be returning Matta now from school. She shrugged on the dishdasha, hanging in loose folds around her slender frame, hiding her gently rounded stomach. No one must know. Matta didn't know and she wanted to keep it that way for as long as possible.

There was a knock at the door. She waited for the housekeeper to open it. She didn't want to meet any of Zahir's men face to face. But then she remembered her housekeeper was in the middle of baking. Anna walked down the tiled hallway to the door, pulling her robe around her.

"Mom!" Matta hugged Anna's legs. Only then did Anna look up, straight into Zahir's eyes—black, cold, and distant. It hurt to see the cold directed to her: eyes that had been so hot for her, but now—nothing.

"Anna."

"Zahir." She clutched her chest, willing herself to keep breathing. "Matta. I think there are fresh cookies in the kitchen. Why don't you go and see?"

Making airplane noises rather than a simple reply, Matta hummed his way out of the room, banging the door behind him.

"What are you doing here?"

"You missed the meeting I requested with you this morning so I've come to you. I want to talk to you about Matta's schooling. I'm not happy with it."

She indicated that he should sit, showing she could be as formal and as icy as he. "Is that right?"

Zahir continued to stand. "His schooling is all wrong."

"In what way?"

"Because it is here in Paris, and not with me in Qawaran."

Shocked, Anna took a step back. She hadn't imagined, for one minute, that he'd wanted to talk to her about taking Matta back to Qawaran. "Ah, a good concrete academic reason then."

"He has to come back with me."

"But we've agreed."

"I've changed my mind."

Anna took a deep breath. Responding in anger or frustration wouldn't get her anywhere. "Please take a seat."

Zahir sat where indicated and Anna carefully sat opposite, her spine ramrod straight so as not to reveal the curves of her stomach.

"Thank you."

"Matta has excellent school reports. He is doing very well and the school has an excellent reputation."

"He is to return with me."

"No. He stays with me." She didn't raise her voice. She wasn't the same, desperate, scared woman as before. And Zahir was to thank for that. "You seem to like playing this game."

"It's no game."

"Then you won't mind if you don't win."

"You know I always win."

Anna decided to ignore the challenge. "Would you like a coffee?"

"Thank you."

She also knew how to play his games now—with decorum but always getting what she wanted. She rose, careful to make sure the gown shrouded her figure and rang the bell before returning, with the same care, back to her hard-backed chair.

"You've been well?" She knew the words, the form to take, whether the questions were required or not. And in this case they weren't. He looked as strong and as handsome as always.

"Yes thank you. And you?"

She nodded, hoping he wouldn't notice the fact that rather than gaining weight during her pregnancy, she'd remained the same with the constant sickness and her face had become thinner. "Yes, I'm well."

"Wearing Qawaranian robes I see. You must have acquired a taste for them."

"They're comfortable."

"You feel free in them I take it."

She nodded. "Yes."

"And freedom is, of course, everything to you. More than your husband, more than your child—"

"Don't come in here and start arguing with me."

"I'm merely describing a truth. It is a truth isn't it?"

It had been, but was no longer. She looked into his eyes

but refused to answer. That he should come to her, after months of silence and pick an argument, infuriated her.

"Anna. Your life—it is as you wanted it to be? Your freedom?"

His voice had become quiet, the brief flare of anger was gone. But she'd wished it remained because without it there was only a stark politeness that meant nothing. There was no sarcasm, no bitterness in his words. He just wanted to know; a polite enquiry.

"Yes. I've always wanted to be free, to be independent, and I am."

He sat back in his chair. She didn't like the way he nodded thoughtfully. She felt her hopes rise. Perhaps he really had come to see her.

"And you?"

He nodded once. "Yes. Everything is going to plan."

"Of course it is."

A heavy silence fell between them. She had to break it, rather than endure his intense gaze.

"So you return tomorrow?"

"It depends."

"Upon what? Not Matta, I hope."

He looked up from beneath lowered lids at her. "No. I will come for him when I am ready. I am not waiting for him."

"Good." Good wasn't adequate word enough to convey the utter relief she felt.

"No. I am waiting upon a woman."

Anna felt sick to her stomach; any newly-born hope that he was here for her was blown away. So there was a woman. "I see."

There was a knock at the door and the housekeeper entered laden with coffee and cake. They both sat in silence while she laid them out. Anna poured a small cup of coffee for Zahir, concentrating on calming her shaking hands, and then one for herself that she didn't touch. Only when the door closed behind the housekeeper did she speak.

"And this woman is proving reluctant?"

"A little. But I know her well and am sure she will have none of the problems you had when first moving to Qawaran."

"Well, that's good for her. And good for you then."

"Yes. But she would benefit by talking to you about it."

"If you need my help then perhaps you're losing your touch."

"No." He leaned forward. "I can assure you she is very receptive to my touch."

Anna willed herself not to feel anything at his words but failed. She drew a deep, unsteady breath to at least stop herself from shaking. Focus, just focus on the words. "Then what? She doesn't want to live in Qawaran?"

"She's unsure at the moment. She needs time to make up her mind." He sat back and sipped his coffee, his eyes never leaving hers. "Perhaps you could speak to her, tell her about the place?"

Pain shot through her limbs from her heart. It was for real. Another woman would step into the life that had been hers and that she'd never cherished as much as she should have done. It was only these past months when she'd gained all that she'd ever said she wanted, that she realized what she'd lost, what she'd never valued, what it was that she really had been wanting all along. But there was no chance of that now.

"What could I tell her that you could not?"

"I think you are the only person she would listen to."

"I'm surprised. I would have thought I'd be the last person."

"No. You are the only person who has experienced what

she will experience. You liked it well enough in Qawaran didn't you?"

She nodded.

"Then you could tell her what you think of the palace as a place to live. What would you tell her?"

She couldn't meet his gaze. It seemed to pierce her through to her very soul. She shifted in her seat. "It's a very satisfactory place."

"Satisfactory? That wouldn't tell her much. She would want to know what it was like."

Anna closed her eyes as she remembered the soaring walls, the light filtering through the ancient corridors, the view that went on forever, the everlasting spring of water that gave life and healing.

"It's magical," she whispered, perspiration prickling her brow. The words seemed to have been wrung out of her. She felt weak. But she couldn't be weak. Not now, not in front of Zahir.

"Good. Then she should have no qualms about living there."

Anna clasped her hands together, her fingers rubbing together as she tried to gather her strength and make sure the robe was pulled out from her stomach.

"I hope that's enough for you?"

"No. She would want to know about the land."

Anna looked down as her mind captured memories of searing heat that shimmered white, playing with mirages of water, horizons of a setting sun shedding its rich light over the expansive landscape; of dry wadis carved by water and time wending their way up into the mountains.

She nodded and swallowed, meeting his gaze. She wouldn't dissemble. The straighter she was, the sooner this horrible interview would be over. "It, too, is magical."

"And the climate?"

Anna felt herself sag. This inquisition seemed to be lasting an age. But she couldn't back out.

"Extreme."

She noticed his face drop slightly at the ambiguous word, as if she suggested criticism.

"You did not enjoy the climate?"

"How could one not enjoy the rain that fell after so much sun; then the light of the sun followed by the brilliance of the stars—" she stopped short.

"Then the people, my family?"

"They are kind. Your new wife will have no problems with them. She will enjoy their company."

"This is sounding most satisfactory. I am sure she will find your words most comforting. Is there anything else I've forgotten? What about me? What would you say about living with me? Do you have any words of advice for her there?"

She looked up into his eyes then, not believing he could drag her through the pain of each element of life living with him, through the eyes of another person.

"I'd tell her—" but she couldn't go on, she heard, and felt, her voice crack.

"Go on."

"You wouldn't want me to speak with her about you."

"Why not?"

"Because I'd tell her the truth about you."

"I am not afraid of the truth." His eyes glittered.

"Yes. She probably realizes already what an arrogant, insensitive bastard you are, who would stop at nothing to get what he wants. Who would even drag his ex-wife—"

"Not yet 'ex'—"

"His ex-wife along to help sweet-talk her into doing what he wants."

"And what would that sweet-talk say? Tell me, Anna, was

I so bad to live with?" He was leaning forward, watching her, his eyes no longer cold, but hot, searing, wanting.

She looked into his eyes, startled. "Bad?" She shook her head, feeling the pricking of tears at the back of her lids. "No. You were—everything. Not good, not bad, just, you."

"Just me. Well, we must hope that is enough for her."

She sagged back into her chair feeling drained but there was one more thing she had to get sorted. "I can't have Matta living in Qawaran being cared for by another woman. I don't know her for God's sake. I can't have it, Zahir, please don't do this again."

"We made a bargain once. And we kept both sides of the bargain. Can I ask, Anna, was your side of the bargain worth it? Your freedom?"

She closed her eyes. "Stop it, Zahir. What is it that you want from me?"

"I want the truth. You have no one to protect now, no reason to not tell me the truth. Do you have what it was that you wanted, what you believed freedom would bring you? Do you?"

How could he even think that she'd enjoyed life away from him these past months? Yes, her studies and Matta and living in Paris had brought joy. But it paled into insignificance by the side of the longing that she'd had to live with. She done what she had to do, but it was like sleep-walking, going through the motions, waiting until you could go back to bed and dream of the man in whose arms you longed to be.

"Yes."

He jumped up and walked to the window.

"And no," she added.

He turned to her then. "Stop playing with me, woman and tell me straight."

"Haven't you learned anything by now? Nothing is straight. Nothing is black and white."

"Some things are, Anna. Some things are."

"So you tell me. Was your side of the bargain worth it? Did you rid yourself of your obsession with me? Are your nights and days peaceful now?"

His jaw ground with a tension that sparked black in his eyes. "You never leave me."

Her lips parted, a thrill went through her body and she swallowed hard.

"I need to know," he continued. "And then I'll leave you forever. Your freedom. Was it worth it all? Is it what you truly want? Was it Anna?" He rose and stood over her, his hands clenching and unclenching as if stopping himself from reaching out. "I need to know."

She licked her dry lips. "Bargaining is such a useful tool."

His frown could have been a weapon in itself. "It is only useful if both have something the other wants."

"Oh, I have what you want. And I'm not talking about Matta."

He came to her then and pushed his fingers through her hair, holding her face tight within his large hands. She could feel their roughness and their tenderness in every sinew of his fingers.

His face was close to hers now, his lips, a breath away. "Tell me what it is that you have, that I want. Tell me now, Anna, before I go crazy."

"This." She breached the slender distance between them and pressed her lips gently to his. Neither moved, simply held the soft touch of their lips, treasuring it, letting the connection flow through their bodies, through every nerve, fiber, muscle, vein, until it filled them both.

They separated then. But the connection was re-made, forged by a kiss. It was in his eyes as he looked at her and it was in her eyes as she gazed upon the one thing freedom had excluded her from, the one man that she couldn't live without.

"I love you Zahir. You make me free. You are all I want."

"Anna." Half-moan, half-groan. She felt her name pressed into her lips as his own found hers in a kiss that breathed life back into her life, gave her back the passion without which she could not live. He pulled away as if suddenly doubting her words. "I love you Anna. You've shown me how to love, you've forced me to look inside myself and find that love. And I have. But are you sure you love me, after all the mistakes I've made, after how I failed you and my brother?"

She smiled at this man, so strong and yet to her now, unafraid to show his true self. "No mistakes, no failings. Just a heart that takes the wrong turn sometimes. Hearts do that."

"Come back to Qawaran with me."

She smiled. "That depends."

"On what?"

"On what kind of bargain I can strike."

"I see. And so in return for your good self, what is it that you want from me?"

"Undying love for me and your children."

"Agreed. I already feel that love for you and Matta."

"I need more than that."

He frowned. "I love you, Anna. I love Matta. I always will. I promise to care for you, to cherish you, to worship you both forever. Isn't that enough?"

She shook her head. "No, I need"—she took his hand and brought it hard against her body, flattening his palm around the edges of her obviously pregnant stomach so he was left in no doubt—"you to love her as well."

He sighed and dropped his forehead against hers. His eyes closed, his hand caressing her stomach without her aid now.

"You're pregnant." He exhaled the words rather than say them and she felt his joy in every nerve ending of her body.

"Yes. I've had a scan. It's a girl."

"A sister for Matta," he murmured as he pressed his lips to hers in a brief kiss. She wanted more but he held her face firm within the palms of his hands, tantalizingly close but not close enough to kiss. She frowned as a smile played on his lips. "It's my turn to be greedy because, Anna, that's not enough for me."

"What do you mean?"

"He'll need a brother, too."

She grinned back. "Of course." She licked her lips. "I take it that the bargain has been struck then," she whispered.

"You take it right," he said as he pulled her to him in a kiss that made her body tremble and her heart fill with joy.

EPILOGUE

Several years later...

Anna lifted her six-week-old second son from her breast and kissed his downy head. She adjusted her clothes and held the sleepy baby up to her nanny's outstretched arms just as Zahir entered the room.

"Zahir! I wasn't expecting you. I thought you would still be in the meeting with those foreign journalists."

He took the baby from the nanny and cradled him in his arms. A lump formed in Anna's throat. Watching Zahir change over the years with each new child they brought into the world moved her. The baby gave a contented little grumble and then promptly fell asleep, nestled in his arms. Zahir stroked his cheek and then looked up at Anna with an expression so full of love it brought tears to her eyes.

"I would have been if it had been me they wanted to speak with. But they're here to see you. The fact that you've opened the first female lawyer's office with branches across the Middle East appears to have made news world-wide."

"Ha!" Anna said triumphantly as she rose and checked

herself in the mirror, pulling her robe into place. "Just as I hoped. It'll focus everyone's attention on legal issues which have been swept out of sight… until now."

She glanced in the mirror at Zahir who was handing back the sleeping babe to his nanny. The door closed behind the nanny and Zahir walked up behind her and put his arms around her waist, pulling her back against his hard body. Desire shot through her and she closed her eyes briefly, allowing the seductive sensations to travel to those parts of her that could never get enough of him. She shifted her head to allow his lips to find the sensitive points of her neck.

"You," he murmured, "have the ability to focus everyone's attention on you." He kissed her again, lower, closer to her breasts that had been made ultra-sensitive through breast-feeding. She moaned and wriggled against his erection. "Mine included," he added. Then he sighed and pulled away. "However, it would seem I have to share you with the world today. They've brought cameras with them. Your work on women's rights and domestic violence has brought you a lot of interest."

She sighed. "Positive and negative interest. I find the negative hard to deal with."

"Of course. But you must remember that I will always have your back, as you say in the US. And, for another, all you have to do is simply speak from your heart and you will win them over."

"My heart? Will that be enough though?"

He turned her in his arms. "Anna, my darling, it will be more than enough." He sighed as he saw her obvious doubt. "Tell me now why it is you've been driven to set up the company."

"You know why."

"Tell me. That way you will keep it in your mind when you meet the journalists."

"Because of what happened to me when I was growing up." She paused. "I want women to know that, whatever their background, wherever they've come from, they can be who they want to be. They can follow their dreams and make those dreams reality."

"Unless their lives are complicated by demanding men." Zahir's tone was light but Anna knew that he regretted his authoritarian manner with her early in their relationship.

She thought about his words as they walked along the corridor, hand-in-hand, to his suite of offices. They paused outside the room where the journalists waited.

"I would have found a way, you know. To leave Qawaran… with Matta. Thing was, my love, I didn't want to. From the first moment I saw you, all those years ago, I knew you were mine, and I was yours." She shrugged. "That was all there was to it. Bottom line." She shrugged. "Of course there were some… *issues* we needed to work through."

He smiled. "And we did, didn't we? And we're the stronger for it." He tucked a strand of hair behind her ear. "Now, are you ready to leave your anonymity behind and step out into the limelight?"

She bit her lip but nodded and stood up straight as he opened the double doors exposing her to a barrage of spotlights and camera flashes. She took a deep breath, smiled and stepped into the full glare of public interest, feeling Zahir's hand lightly on the small of her back. She smiled at the cameras, knowing he was right. He'd always be there for her and she could face anything with the strength of his love behind her.

The End

AFTERWORD

Thank you for reading *The Sheikh's Bargain Bride*. I hope you enjoyed it! Reviews are always welcome—they help me, and they help prospective readers to decide if they'd enjoy the book.

This is the second book in the Desert Kings series:

> Wanted: A Wife for the Sheikh
> The Sheikh's Bargain Bride
> The Sheikh's Lost Lover
> Awakened by the Sheikh
> Claimed by the Sheikh
> Wanted: A Baby by the Sheikh

The third book—*The Sheikh's Lost Lover*—features Razeen and Lucy (excerpt follows). Here's a review of *The Sheikh's Lost Lover* to give you a taste of what to expect.

"It was full of magic, romance and wonderful characters that help

you connect with the story easily. This is one of my most dear stories about sheiks. I TOTALLY recommend it." (iBooks US)

For more information about my books and to sign up to my newsletter, please check out my website: www.dianafraser.com.

Happy reading!

Diana

THE SHEIKH'S LOST LOVER

BOOK 3 OF DESERT KINGS—RAZEEN

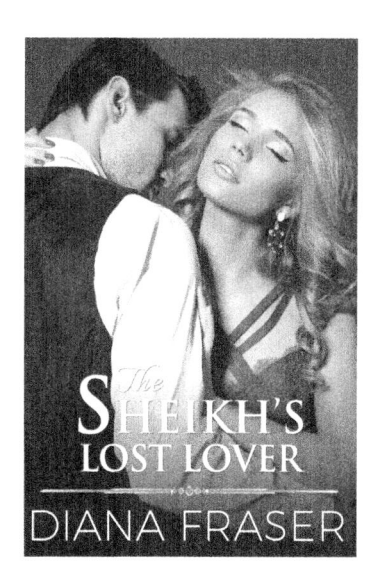

A love affair that must not last...

Lucy Gee sails to Sitra to find her missing sister, Maia, who was last seen in the arms of the King. Lucy doesn't do long-term rela-

tionships, but when she meets the King she falls for him hard. She just has to control her attraction long enough to find Maia, but not long enough so she loses her heart. Two weeks should do it.

Sheikh Razeen ibn Shad was never meant to be King. But, with his father and brother both dead, he's determined to do his duty, even if it means entering into an arranged marriage with a Sitran Princess to gain the approval of his countrymen. But he has two weeks before he has to choose a wife. Two weeks in which to have an affair with Lucy. What could go wrong?

Excerpt

King Razeen ibn Shad looked across the calm waters of the bay, silvered under the light of the bright moon, and watched his old friend climb aboard the yacht. It had been a good night: dinner and conversation with someone who wasn't his employee or his subject, someone who didn't want something from him. The shared laughter and memories made the loneliness afterwards even harder to bear. But he had no choice. His country had to come first.

He was about to turn away when a flash of white on the calm waters drew his attention. He narrowed his eyes and saw a swimmer: arms cutting through the sea in a sleek action designed to move fast through water, designed not to disturb the calm surface, designed not to be seen. And it would have worked if he hadn't been watching so closely.

He moved to the shadow of the palm trees that fringed the beach and watched the faint movement on the water come closer. The beach was off-limits until the scientific survey of the coral reef his friend was undertaking was complete. Until then, no one had permission to be here. Last time they'd had intruders, they'd lost part of the coral forever. He'd make sure it didn't happen again.

Lucy stepped out of the sea onto the still-warm sand, squeezed the water out of her long hair and walked up the beach. After a day spent preparing food below decks, she'd needed a swim—and what a swim. The water was as warm as the soft air that now caressed her body. She breathed deeply of the fragrant air and looked around.

The beach was a perfect crescent of white sand under the sheltering sweep of the palm trees. On one side of the small bay a rocky promontory jutted into the water, marking the beginning of the coral reef the scientists on the boat were here to study and on the other side she could see the uneven outline of mangrove trees.

She'd traveled all over the world but nowhere came close to the perfection of this unspoiled place. The white sand was almost luminous under the starlight and three-quarters moon. The beach was empty: no lights, no people and no sound but the distant hoot of an owl and the seductive splash and drag of the waves. She was quite alone. The only sign of habitation was a low-lying mansion in a neighboring bay and the yacht, bobbing lazily out near the reef.

Perfect. Or it would have been if she didn't have to set her plan into action the next day.

[Buy Now!](#)

∼

ALSO BY DIANA FRASER

The Mackenzies

The Real Thing

The PA's Revenge

The Marriage Trap

The Cowboy's Craving

The Playboy's Redemption

The Lakehouse Café

New Zealand Brides

Yours to Give

Yours to Treasure

Yours to Cherish

Desert Kings

Wanted: A Wife for the Sheikh

The Sheikh's Bargain Bride

The Sheikh's Lost Lover

Awakened by the Sheikh

Claimed by the Sheikh

Wanted: A Baby by the Sheikh

Italian Romance

Perfect

Her Retreat

Trusting Him

An Accidental Christmas

Printed in Great Britain
by Amazon